98 Wounds

98 Wounds
Justin Chin

Manic *D* Press
San Francisco

In Memoriam

E. Brian Shelley
Cheryl B.

The author wholeheartedly thanks Dave Thomson, Zack Linmark, Lisa Asagi, Faye Kicknosway, Lori Takayesu, Lüch Linmark & Greg Boorsma, my lovely family, Michelle Tea, Ali Liebegott & Beth Pickens at Radar Productions, Radar Lab 2010, Jen Joseph & Manic D Press, the San Francisco Foundation Fund for Artists, all the writers & artists & oddbits who kindly & magnanimously donated of their time & work & moxie to the fundraising auction efforts & especially to all the donors for their generosity & support.

Slightly different versions of some works contained herein have previously appeared in the following publications: *Flesh & The Word 4* (Plume), *Porn*, (Harrington Park), *Best of the Best Gay Erotica 1996-2000* (Cleis), *Best Gay Erotica 1997* (Cleis), *ZYZZYVA*. Vol XIII, No. 2 & Vol XV, No. 3, and *580 Split*. Issue 9.

Published by Manic D Press. For information, contact Manic D Press, PO Box 410804, San Francisco CA 94141   www.manicdpress.com
Printed in Canada

Library of Congress Cataloging-in-Publication Data

Chin, Justin, 1969-
98 wounds / Justin Chin.
   p. cm.
ISBN 978-1-933149-57-8 (pbk. original) -- ISBN 978-1-933149-37-0 (ebook)
I. Title.
PS3553.H48973A616 2011
   811'.54--dc23

               2011031510

Contents

Apologies, repentance, failure, and defeat are always so much better when in the form of a story

Outsider

The hiking was just too much, he thought. The camping in and of itself was tolerable; and the rafting he grudgingly admitted was even a little bit fun, but the paddle-boating, the kayaking, the rambling, the rock climbing, the all-terrain biking, and the hiking, oh lord, the hiking was just too much. All this outsiderness is just so tedious and so exhausting, he thought. Okay, it might be gorgeous out there, but he was content to enjoy that beauty conceptually.

And the outside was teeming with things that just wanted to eat you. Even if they had to do it in tiny little bites, they wanted to devour you. It just seems such an itchy place to put oneself. Even our ancestors knew better: they were cavemen, because they had caves.

And who decided that such a lifestyle epitomizes health? That participating in such activities proved the strength of a person's mental and physical character? In advertisements for pharmaceutical drugs, they often show the presumably diseased person hanging off a precipice all muscles and sweat, or mountain biking in lycra shorts and asymmetrical sunglasses. All that to signify Power and Strength and Healing.

Do we not have enough in our lives that give us ample opportunities to display the content of our characters? To display strength?

Try negotiating with health insurance companies, or that same pharmaceutical company, or your indifferent and egomaniacal physician who has spent a considerable amount of time and money on his degree and will not be questioned nor told otherwise by some diseased slut. Try dealing with an insane and despotic boss. Try to resume living normally after your heart has been irrevocably broken by whichever of the multitude of ways that hearts break. Try scratching that grey itch, only to realize it's really ringworm.

There, there. Come inside. You don't have to prove anything here.

Quietus

"How would you like to die?" he asks.

"How anyone would," I say. "In my sleep, in my own bed." I could turn the question around back to him but the answer was, if not obvious, then at least suspended in our air. So I say instead, "How would you *not* like to die? What's the worst death?"

"Anything involving lava, or quicksand," he says.

"Is there still quicksand? Didn't the U.N. and the World Health Organization eradicate that in the late '60s?"

"No, they gave up after polio and smallpox," he says. "Your worst death?"

"Animals," I say. "Being eaten by some wild hungry animal. What would be really awful is if the animal had a small jaw, and so it has to take lots of little bites to finish you off."

"On the flip side of that, can you imagine being mauled by panda bears?" he says. "Wouldn't that be the cutest death ever?"

"Or else," I offer, "a headline in the newspapers might read: *Autopsy reveals that man killed by three-toed sloth actually died of late stage cancer.*"

A week ago, we watched a TV movie on cable called *Strays*. A family – father, mother, young child, and newly born infant – moves into their dream home out in the woodsy suburbs. And then the nightmare begins. They are stalked by a colony of feral cats. The alpha male cat, the principal evil who's supposedly afraid of water (obviously), looked like he had been dipped in a bucket of K-Y Jelly and barely towel dried. The tag line for the movie was *Cats have nine lives, you only have one.* There was a lot of clawing and scratching and more clawing until their victims inexplicably died. And not to mention with inflamed sinuses, too. I believe one victim even threw himself off the third floor balcony to his death just so the awful mewing and clawing would stop.

It's a cliché in horror movies when, during a suspenseful moment, a cat would suddenly fly, or rather be flung, screeching and meowing across the screen. In this movie, however, that tired ruse made perfect sense and it happened quite frequently as well.

"What's the collective noun for cats?" he asks.

"A bunch of cats? A furby of cats? A plié of cats? An allergy of cats?" I say guessing, but he's already dozed off. Then, now, it's darkening in gradual sheets outside and in here, and he's getting tired. When I leave, I will go to his apartment and attempt to tidy up, put things away, pack things up. What more can I do? Twelve days ago he left for his medical specialist's appointment and never came back, sent straight to hospice care, and his apartment is evidence of that. Everything – every object and piece of furniture, every wall hanging and scrap of paper, every appliance and implement, every book and record, every withering houseplant and all the pillows on the bed, even the air aswirl with particles of dust and dander – hangs as if in mid-sentence. It's a kind of heartbreak I never knew I could or would ever recognize.

It is mid-day, an ordinary unsurprising type of mild any day, when I get an text message from him which reads *This is kind of it, kiddies. I'm feeling one fry short of the Happiest Meal. I feel like I'm underwater more and more each hour. Thank you for everything. You are all precious to me.*

A whole lot of cats is a clowder, a clutter, a cluster, a colony, a glorying, a pounce, a kindle, a litter, a dout, a parliament, a seraglio, a glaring, a destruction.

You can't just create a scale of humanity to suit your own ends...
Either we're all damned or we're all saved – end of story.
— Neal Drinnan, *Izzy and Eve*

Burn

He has fallen asleep, passed out, is snoring like the last hog on earth, sweating like a lost marathon runner. His white t-shirt is drenched, the sheets and the pillows are drenched with his sweat. I want to sleep but cannot. I paw him, run my hands over his wet body but he cannot wake as I cannot sleep. I wipe his sweat off on my chest, I pull his shirt up and rub my face into his sweaty belly. I adore everything that comes out of his pores, his bitter toxic sweat, his stinky overheated body.

Our love is bound by chemicals. How I hold my arm out to him and let him run the line into my vein. How beautiful my blood looks as it surges into the syringe, like a rare flower blossoming, and how beautiful it feels as he pumps it, chemical rich, back into me. While he runs his line, I put my finger on the small blood spot, pinprick in flesh where the needle plunged in, and press it to stop the bleeding, I hold my arm up so the blood will flow right. He has his arm up as well as we are like monkeys at the zoo, monkey see, monkey do; we are legs and arms and mouths and primate rough.

We fuck unsafe. The first time, whenever that was, I sat straddled on his lap, reached down, pulled the condom off him and stuffed him right back inside of me. The next time when I fucked him, and the next time he fucked me, and the next time we fucked, we never thought of rubber. We thought of sweat and cum and spit and piss. We thought of a gooey elastic ball of faggot sex.

We never thought of cash or time, and they were fast running out.

"Why do you do this? We can get you help. You're sick, sick." Mom is distraught. "I taught you better. Don't tell your grandmother, it'll kill her. Wait till your dad finds out, he'll kill you." Mom is crying. "Where did I go wrong? Is it the friends you hang out with? Why don't you go to church, pray to God to help you? I don't know who you are anymore, you are not my son." Mom is enraged. "Why? Why? Why?" Mom is sad and powerless.

All so TV movie-of-the-week, so After-school Special Program pre-empting *Oprah* and *Days*. Except in the TV movie, I steal her handbag and ransack it in a dirty alleyway for twenty dollars and buy badly cut drugs from Escobar. In the TV movie, I end up as a hooker, living in the bus station, beat up by druggies masquerading as cops, jump off the roof of a tenement building, get all sorts of venereal diseases, write poems and save my life; there are heroic social workers, good cops, tearful forgiveness scenes, and Emmy-worthy redemption scenes scored with cheesy music, maybe even intervention by angels. In the TV movie twelve years ago, instead of poems, I would have found breakdancing as salvation.

But this is not TV. I walk out and Mom is still crying in the kitchen, the dinner preparations stopped, the dishes in the sink unwashed. Pity, I was going to help her wash the dishes and do the rice in the cooker, I'm a whizz at that, knowing how much water to put into the pot, how to measure with the knuckles of my finger, but not when she is in such a state.

On a two-day high, the best time of the ride, we are driving in the truck. "Look, car wash," he points to the parking lot of a small church. On the chain link fence, a tatty poorly made banner announces "Youth Challenge Car Wash $5" in fluorescent primary colors. I pull into the lot and into a parking spot, and six teenagers trot towards the truck with hoses, pails, and rags in tow. While they soap and hose the car down, we wait in the refreshment tent. Mild coffee, fruit punch, and cookies. The group leader comes over. "How's the car wash been going?" I ask.

He says it's slow, that they do this every week, that they're raising money to send the kids to Woodside for a "real fun" summer camp. The leader is a beefy, suburban-looking guy, might be of Mexican or Central American heritage, and swaggers in that Big Brothers of America sort of way. The way mentors are supposed to swagger, that walk that says, "I've been there, bro, but I got out. I saw the light, I had (pick one) Jesus+God / The Blessed Virgin / Education / Scientology / Good Sense / Visions of Death / All of the Above. Yeah, I've been there. Gangs and drugs are a downhill slide (or an uphill battle)." Apparently an uphill battle and a downhill slide, though both diametrically opposite like parallel train tracks that will never cross, are really the same thing metaphorically. And an uphill slide is, well, technically impossible except at the Mystery Spot in Santa Cruz. But they were saving the lives of youth-at-risk here, youth-of-color-at-risk no less, no time for semantic squabbles.

I am getting antsy. The high is coursing through me and I want to be somewhere right now fucking. We both have our sunglasses on even though it is a cloudy day, we are both twitchy and sweating. If Mr. Leader had done his time, he would know that we were high as Mr. and Mr. Kite. Even a blind social worker could see that from across two orphanages.

"It's a good thing," he says. "Kids these days need so much help staying out of trouble. God knows if I had car washes and camp in my day, I would have turned out different."

"You did have car washes and camp," I say. "We all had car washes and camps."

"Oh, yeah," he says. "I guess I should have gone to car washes and camp." And we giggle and guffaw like idiots. Mr. Leader looks at us in bewilderment. We hear the car horn beep and one of the kids is waving at us.

"All finished!" he yells. The truck is shiny spankingly clean.

"Good job," I tell the kid and hand him a twenty. The spotty teenager grins and thanks us, and the other kids all chime in their thank you's, visions of birds and trees and camping gear dancing in their bright eyes.

"God bless you," we hear Mr. Leader call to us as we drive out of the lot.

In the rear-view mirror, I can see the kids swarm over another car like ants over a half-chewed M&M. These kids will not be like us. They will be saved. They will have clear thoughts and proud parents and adoring siblings. They will be something. They may one day even meet the President of the United States. Heck, one of them might even *be* the President of the United States, and in his inauguration speech he will retell of those weeks of car washes and those summers of camps. He will remember the car with two guys who gave a twenty and it showed him how much the American people were good people who wanted to help the less fortunate.

He pulls open the ashtray and starts laughing. "I left a small bag of pot here, two good fat joints. It's gone."

"Maybe they vacuumed it up."

"There wasn't a vacuum, they didn't do the inside of the car, they only washed the outside."

"Maybe one of the kids found it and decided to turn it in to their chief, do his good deed and turn his back on Satan."

"Or maybe some kids have found a way to get through washing cars all day."

"You didn't leave it there intentionally, did you?"

He smiles so sweetly and rummages in his shirt pocket. "You want a hit?" He holds his finger coated with speed up to my nose and I snort what I can in, suck off what's left on his finger. Later he will coat his finger and stick it in my arse and the burn will last for hours as he fucks me.

I imagine a house with a thatched roof by the sea with primroses, bougainvilleas, and tuberoses in the garden. It is a cute little bungalow, with a homely kitchen, a fireplace, a big bed, good stuff. We wake and sleep each night with the crash of surf. On warm nights, the smell of the pikake flowers permeates everything, and it is on such nights that our lovemaking is infused with a certain drenched frenzy. I make sumptuous meals in the kitchen. He goes to work in the late morning and returns in the afternoon. I tend to the garden in the backyard, growing two kinds of lettuce, cabbage, spinach (Chinese and Euro), tomatoes, potatoes, carrots, chard, parsley, basil, chillies, sweet peppers. Sometimes we fish and catch beautiful luscious snappers or whitefish. We go to the local store for meats and milk, trade with our neighbors four miles away who raise free-range fowl. At the end of summer, we can see seals and sea lions on the beach; at the end of spring, there are whales far in the sea. Sitting on the deck, we can see the sprays of water gushing out of their whale-holey-things as their black-gray bodies playfully lunge out of the sea. There is a well-worn brick fireplace in the living room and every week we pick up driftwood and fallen twigs for firewood. We sit in front of the dry crackle in big comfy armchairs, have tea and fresh-baked biscuits and read books and listen to the stereo. There is a big, good-natured, well-trained shaggy dog, of course, and what the hell, let's also have a cat who solves mysteries. Friends come around once in a while for tea or dinner, but mostly for brunch. The seagulls outside are considerate and never poop on the property; we reward them with little sardines and pieces of cut-up cuttlefish. There are few other people in the world but us it seems. All through summer and autumn, there are mad meteor showers in the night sky, so many shooting stars but we have stopped wishing for anything because we have everything we ever need and want.

We have each other and this house by the beach, but it is an apartment on the third floor and it faces another dismal dirty apartment building, and it is filled with the acrid ether smoke from the crack pipe. The crack at the bottom of the door is stuffed with cat piss stained bath towels. The shades are drawn and porno is on the TV. We have not bathed in days. He smells like crude sweat and stale piss and I love that smell on him. I think I must smell like that, too, as he burrows his nose into my armpit and arse crack. We jerk our flaccid penises until they are raw; tie our genitals up with rope and cock-straps that rub the underside of our scrotums to blisters, all to achieve erections that last for four minutes at the most; we drink water and diluted Gatorade and beers, piss it out on each other and in each other's arses, letting the bitter chemical slush recycle into the bloodstream of the rectum. We ejaculate, after much effort, our watery cum onto each other. We wonder what time it is. How much more there is in the pipe. Where we can get some more. How will we get some more. When to take a break. When to stop to take our medications. When the insurance check will run out, or the disability payments will stop. When the dealer will get busted or O.D. When to start again and how.

Soon the come-down will happen. The cramps, the stiff joints, the sore muscles, the aching jaws, and the long dead sleep will take over. There's nothing more comforting when coming down than cheap Mexican food or take-away soup from the Chinese restaurant down the street because our jaws and teeth and gums are too sore to chew and all we can do is swallow like trained seals at Marine World.

Do you hear voices in your head? *No. What voices? I do not. What the hell are you talking about?* Do you hear a droning sound inside your brain? *No, I hear a symphony and it's playing a melody for you and me.* Do you find yourself doing things you have no consciousness of? *Only when I'm baking, Martha Stewart reports going into a trance state when she is baking with her cast-iron cookware, and she emerges from that trance with a tray of tasty sweets and doughy nut breads dusted in vanilla-scented confectioners' sugar.* Do you wake up and wonder where you are? *I am always where I am.* Are you afraid of bright lights? *On the contrary, I seek out bright lights because I love wearing dark glasses to look at my tall, thin shadow. After last call at the bar, I turn myself towards the fluorescent lights in the ceiling like some night-blooming sunflower waiting to photosynthesize in the moonlight.* Do you feel things crawling on your skin? *I have dry skin and moisturizing constantly is a pain.* Tell me what do you see? *I see nothing I am not supposed to see.* Do you hear voices telling you to do bad things? *I don't know what bad things are.* Oh, come on now, everybody knows what bad things are.

It was the first time we ever played. We played chemical from Day One for four days and we crashed together. Fell asleep and when I woke in his apartment with him, I knew he was the one. I had never crashed with anyone before; that I prefer to do on my own, in my own time, it is not a pretty sight. But as I woke with him and he with me, we knew that this was it. If you can wake from your crash with the person you played with and still want that person. If you are not repulsed, sick, sickened, anxious to be somewhere else. If you ever entertained the thought of playing clean with that person then you are in more trouble than you can imagine.

This man.

The floors of the Forbidden City in China are tiled with concrete slabs seventeen layers thick. Workers, indentured servants, slaves, and prisoners were forced to work year after year, generations enslaved to lay slab upon slab of stone to protect the emperor from evil conscienceless assassins who schemed to burrow under the palace, tunnel through the floors and break into the emperor's room and stab him in his heart, slay without a careless thought. So it is with my love for him. I will peel away each layer, chip at the granite and marble, make him a maze through the underground, through the layers of cynicism and hurt, dig through the crusty bits of grief so that he may enter easily even as I sleep, and once there, he shall be the emperor of my heart.

Coming down from a six-day high, I come home in the morning to the phone message machine blinking devilishly and a message from my aunt to go visit my mother in the hospital.

I wash my face, and take a cab to General. Mom is lying in the bed with tubes, catheters, picc-lines and wires plugged into her. Everything smells chemical, medicinal, antiseptic, clean. It is the smell of healing, even though the chances are fifty-fifty or perhaps even less. She is lying in her blue hospital smock and lying back on the few flat pillows they provide and what Dad or an aunt has snagged from another room. She opens her eyes weakly when I enter.

She smiles, she is genuinely happy to see me.

"How are you feeling?" I ask, which is always the stupidest question ever though that seems to be the universal default in such situations.

She says she's okay, but she is not. The cancer has spread. She is in pain even with the morphine drip, she hurts like nothing I can imagine, even as my own body is aching like I've been torqued in some sadistic gym machine.

Mom is lying there without her make-up on and the lines in her face are showing. Mom and make-up were always a twin deal. "There are no ugly girls, just lazy ones," her pearl of wisdom she imparted to my sisters and girl cousins, extolling the virtues of lipsticks, blushes, eyeshadows and eyeliners, all to a wave of rolled eyeballs. Mom's idea of perfect make-up is the panstick of Mary Kay and Avon ladies. Merle Norman was her goddess. But here she is, lying in pain and make-up-less; frankly I always thought she looked better without all that make-up on. But her face shows such exhaustion. And in the reflection in the stainless steel implements in the room, I can see how tired I look too.

I pull up a chair and sit beside her, and I make my excuses: I had a project due. I had an out-of-town work assignment. I keep missing the window of visiting hours. Can she see the lies? They say parents always know. My siblings have all been in and out all week, on a schedule, a rotation that nobody even bothered to include me in or inform me of. I put my hand over hers. I'm not sure which of ours is colder or clammier. "You look tired," she says. "You look so tired and so thin."

"I'm okay. I'm not. Don't start to nag now." I can hear myself getting slightly irritated and try to tamp it down a notch, try to sound good-natured and jokey. What the hell is wrong with me?

"Okay," she says. She senses that kernel of irritation, she's seen it bloom and explode into such ugliness so many times in our life, she's jousted against it so many times in the past but not now. Her tone turns apologetic. "It's just that I worry about you a lot."

"Mom! We're can all take care of ourselves. You don't need to worry." *Don't sound pissy. Be a normal fucking child for once, you shit. Be good. Be nice.*

"Mothers will always worry." I have heard her say this so many times, even as I know that soon I'll never hear it said ever again. "When you all were small, when you were younger, Dad and I, sometimes...."

I put my head down on the side of the bed to rest my head. I am tired, so fucking tired, and I don't want to see Mom like this. I want to see her in the kitchen roasting a chicken, sewing new curtains, working the salad shooter, going to church, arguing with Dad and me and my brother, gardening, plotting a trip to Australia and coming home with tacky souvenirs. She puts her hand on my head and strokes my head. My grandma lived with us when I was in preschool and during afternoon nap-time she would lie beside me and stroke my head and tickle my ear until I fell asleep. With Mom stoking my head, I feel like a little kid again.

I wake with a start. I must have fallen asleep. Mom is sleeping quietly. It is late afternoon. I walk out of the hospital and head home, fingering the lighter in my pocket. It is a cigar lighter, a name brand no less, a heavy chrome thing that fires a fierce blue flame. It's great for pipes since it burns cleaner and hotter. I go home, dig my pipe out of the bedside drawer, fire the lighter up, and smoke what's left in the pipe until the glass bulb is clean. The smoke burns exquisitely into my cheeks and into my lungs, and the familiar bile-like taste fills my mouth and throat, and I can feel my energy returning. I wipe the lighter clean, it was something a trick left behind. I scrape together a couple of watches, some useless electronics. I head over to the pawn shop and bargain with the proprietor. In the end, he gives me a decent price. I head on past all the junkies, whores, and dealers on the street until I reach Church Street where I pop into the flower store. I buy a spray of flowers. Orchids, tulips, lilies, irises, a twig or two of cherry blossoms or was it pussy willows? The fey guy behind the counter graciously wraps the whole thing with greens and binds it beautifully with a rattan twine. I pop into the deli nearby and buy a small bag of the pineapple jam tarts that Mom likes so much, and head on back to the hospital. She is still sleeping when I return. I want her to wake to her favorite snack and a big colorful living vibrant thing in her room. To awaken to a loveliness and a treat, the way her life should have been, and not the haggard reminder of disappointment and worry that I've heaped on her for so long.

I look at Mom in the yellow setting sunlight that is peeking through the blinds. Her face is pale, and it really has been a long time since I have seen her without her make-up. The thing about her face are her eyebrows. She had them tattooed on years ago – "now I don't ever have to worry about penciling or plucking anymore," she announced – and now she is lying here, her face is truly drawn and tired and I see how sick she really is, sicker than ever, and she is all eyebrows, eyebrows, thick dark painted-on sharp-edged eyebrows.

Somedays, I want to just disappear, escape to somewhere. Get in the car and drive, live out that Bruce Springsteen song and every other Springsteen song about driving on the heck outta there. I have two months back-rent to pay, the bills are piling up, the highs are higher, and the lows are no worse than they have ever been, my health is shorting out. I want to have a normal life, whatever that may be, and whether I'm even capable of that or not is questionable. I want to be a good man, a good man to more than one man. I want to know how to do this.

We are still in mad love. We are in the truck headed for Pismo Beach, inspired by the Bugs Bunny cartoon. He is sleeping, breathing roughly, slumped against the car door, the seat-belt cutting into his cheek. My brain is telling me to stay awake, that I will be all right. My body is telling me that it is shutting down fast. My arm is twitching, my elbow hurts. I am afraid that I'm driving blind, about to fall asleep at the wheel. I look at the dashboard. There's half a tank of gas; it's enough to get us there.

Goo

You have the kind of cum that I like, thick yet fluid without the strange lumps that plague some ejaculates, a nice fine blend. Mine, on the other hand, has the consistency of the unnamed white stuff that you might find on tables in vegetarian restaurants. Walking down the street with you, people assume that I'm your little boy. Would they be surprised to know you let me put you on a leash and take you to public restrooms where men suck each other at urinals and masturbate each other under partitions leaving their jism in careless splatters on the tiled floors? You obediently go down on all fours and lap up the spatter, some turned liquid, some grey with shoeprint tracks, left by men whose urges have long subsided and gone.

I call you on the phone and you rush to a designated restroom in a quiet office building where I have procured a decent puddle of cum for you. I place the collar on your fleshy neck with the spikes turned inward, attach the heavy chain to it, both pieces picked out by you, and take you to sex clubs and adult bookstores where you dash about like a naughty puppy, vigorously licking at every spot of cum you find. Often I have to jerk on the chain to calm you down.

I take my task with some amount of gravity and would like to take you on a good methodical sweep of the premises, you would prefer to dash at every glob that you spy in any corner.

No, people would not assume anything of that sort when they see how you rush to buy me drinks at bars, how dapper you look in your expensive clothes, how you fawn over me and hold my hand at the symphony. Your slowly receding hairline, your slightly paunchy belly, the lines in your face starting to show, your homosexual cravings sure. You look like a kindly uncle, an older professor indulging in some non-academic fancies.

You are a connoisseur of your craving; you approach each spot of cum as if you were a zoologist in search of some elusive animal: this one was spat out, this was flicked from a hand, this one tried to dash to the safe place to prevent a mess, this was in a rush, this hadn't cum in days. How much of this is fancy I do not question. This one went to the market, this one cried wee-wee-wee all the way home.

Once I told you my theory of Mormons and how their cum would taste somehow different because Mormons were the human equivalents of range-free chicken. All that clean living and loose underwear must have some effect on those testicles, and you promised me that you would find out the truth about Mormon cum.

Once, just once, we stumbled upon a rare find, something you never found again: a mid-sized puddle of cum with a spot of blood in it, perhaps the poor bloke had a bladder or urethral nick, perhaps there were bleeding gums. You put your face so close to the pool and instead of your usual vigor you very slowly dipped the tip of your tongue into the spooge. You took more than five minutes to finish lapping that small puddle. After that, you developed a deep fear of your craving and you wrote fifteen letters to sex advice columnists in several magazines and newspapers asking for some counsel. For weeks, you scanned the columns trying to find your letter, but the letters were always the same: small dicks, large dicks, burst condoms, fear of intimacy, can't find small enough dicks, can't find large enough dicks, regrettable sex, want to do something the other doesn't and vice versa. You took this as a sign that all was well and your deviance was well within the range of normal deviances and in celebration of this epiphany I took you on another feeding.

Once, in a private moment, I asked you what those puddles of jism tasted like, if each was in some way better than the other, if I should lead you to fresh splotches and forgo the ones sitting for so long till they become indistinguishable from snot. Your answer surprised me, you said they all tasted the same. It tasted of all the men you never had, you said. The urgency in your voice scared me, and I told you I had a dream about nachos.

You tell me I am a faggot piece of shit and that I do not deserve your dick. You snap your finger and point to your boot. I go down and lick the tip of your shoe, allow you to step on my face, to cram the tip of your boot down my mouth. You reward me by spitting into my mouth and fucking my mouth in slow, sharp thrusts. On my knees when I look up at you, you purse your lips and a gleam of spit forms on your mouth that I take willingly into my mine. Sucking your dick, my mouth fills with the sour sting of your piss that I choke down. I let you pinch my nipples until they hurt for days.

I adore your large-balled fists as they smack across my head, each blow a token of your affection and my worthlessness. I teach you how to cut into my flesh with a sharp knife like so many words. You say that I am your dog and I say *less than that*. You wrap your big hands around my neck, I have seen how you snap barbequed beef ribs into two at dinner tables, a messy display of strength to split a piece of yummy treat for us to share. You close your hands around my small neck, my face turns red, I cum hard and you eat the jism off my hands, off my thighs, and off the floor like a gentle goat at the petting zoo.

With my hand up your arse, I can feel the strange squish of your colon in my gloved hand insulating me from your body temperature. The rubber glove, cool against my palm, not long enough to shield my forearm from your warm sphincter and the blood and juices staining my arm a medicinal pink, the color of fresh kill. I uncurl my fist and snap it close again like a sea anemone inside of you; I run my arm in and out of you as if I were digging crab traps on a soft, low tide beach.

You wince when I grab the nub in your pelvis where your spinal cord ends, a hard lump that hides bundles of nerves and arteries, the stuff that tragic car accidents and snapped bungee cords are made of. With my free hand I caress the front of your body, fingering the nipples embedded in your hairy chest, running my hand down the bristly extent of your body, I say hoarse, *Breathe, relax. Take a deep breath.* But whatever you have punching your heart through your bloodstream doesn't even allow you that comfort and I refuse to take my hand out of you even as you plead with me to. I lean over to place your cock in my mouth and you say *Bite my dick.* I clench my teeth down in the middle of your shaft, I draw your foreskin under my teeth and nip into the elastic flaps, you flinch and bear down on my fist sweaty from the heat of your body and the tight non-porous constraints of the rubber glove. I pull my hand out, turn the glove inside out, and hold it up to you. The insides of the glove now filled with traces of your shit and anal slime stained by your internal ruptures. You slip your hand into the glove, retrieve your fluid insides and devour it like a stupid dog that would slurp at anything in front of it. I wipe off the bloodied mucus from my forearms on your back and go home to my cat, my computer, my books.

You put on your clothes, clean up, and return to your lover, your ex-wife and kids and job and politics and upper income life, you call to make plans to meet again, you drop everything when I call you, you do everything I tell you, you buy me gifts and take me to places I cannot afford to go, you tell me your problems with life, work, and love, I listen and make no judgments nor comment, I feed you my cum on occasion though you never ask for it and I seldom offer, and with each tender caress, each deeply done kiss, we slowly become the objects of our hate so much that we wish for nothing more than to see the other dead.

The path is different for everyone... Drugs will take some people directly to Heaven, others to Hell. Some, to both over time. Your body is your temple and how you choose to worship amongst your own congregation is entirely up to you.
—Neal Drinnan, *Izzy and Eve*

Sugar

The diarrhea had gotten so bad that fucking his ass was like poking at an overfilled water-balloon with the jagged-edged finger of a chronic nail-biter. He knew this would happen, it always does. He needed help and he needed help fast. No bulking agents for this boy. He wanted something hard, something that would score his ass. He ended up at his dealer's. At any point of your life, you might have to have sex with your dealer, so it helps to have a dealer you wouldn't mind having sex with.

He is in a dingy residential hotel. Sitting in his underwear on the edge of the scant mattress. He feels the fleas or mites, something, biting him underneath his thighs, he thinks he can feel them burrowing into the elastic band, setting their nests. His dealer is arranging and measuring the baggies. Scattered on the bed is an assortment of dildos and buttplugs. Sticky half-used bottles of lube – some with dust balls and lint, matted twines of fur and stringy hairs stuck to them – litter the bed, too. His dealer lets him take a small hit from the glass pipe. But there are no small hits really, only ravenous gulps of air, and whatever might be in it. He wants more. He can feel his bowels solidifying. This is good, he thinks.

"You see this dildo?" the dealer says, pointing to one of the large fleshy disembodied cocks on the bed.

"Yeah," he says. He swallows another hit.

"It's big, huh? You think you can take it in your ass?"

"It is a little too big for me," he says.

"Well, if you want anything at all, if you want me to give you anything at all, you will let me put it in you. Fuck you with it."

He thinks for a while. He takes another hit. He takes his prepared shot. He agrees.

He lies on his back with his legs spread apart. The hit is prickling right through his body. He can feel it spread through him as if every capillary was trying to go neon. This must be what it feels like to be pickled, what a beetroot or an onion or a cucumber undergoes, he thinks this funny.

The dealer is lubing the dildo. He grabs a bottle of lube and squirts some of the tacky fluid onto his fingers, smears it onto the ass. He runs a finger or two into the ass to loosen it up.

He can feel the warm slush of his shit still there.

The dealer pokes at the butthole with the head of the dildo. The butthole puckers up. The dealer pokes at it with a bit more force.

He tries to loosen up, and the hits he has taken is helping. Poppers, he thinks. That will open everything up. White Rabbits would fall through. Rosebud would not be the name of his sled.

The dealer mercifully changes tactics and proceeds with a smaller training butt-plug. The dealer pushes the butt-plug into the ass.

He breathes in the right moment and motion, and the cruel projectile slips in but not without some sharp pain.

The dealer lets him have another hit, a good big beautiful deep one while twisting the butt-plug around.

His hole feels looser, but he's not sure. He's sure he's had much bigger things up there before but he also knows that one shouldn't live in the past.

The dealer pulls the butt-plug out. And again, he breathes at the right moment and the pain is assuaged in that breath. He can feel some liquid seeping out of his hole. He decides that he will describe it as *glacially oozing* if he ever tells anyone of this night. But it is the middle of the afternoon. Or early morning. Or daylight savings. *Oh, what is the time, Mr. Wolf?*

The dealer doesn't seem to mind the shit, nor does he seem to care; he will leave that room in that residential hotel that night and move to another room somewhere else. The dealer is wielding the evil dildo again, and trying to work it into the ass.

He is torn between wanting to have that huge dildo, huger than any he has ever seen (though he is not in full possession of any senses of perception or perspective), inside of him, fulfill the bargain, get his stuff, and wanting to hold all that shit inside of him, not let it go. He thinks of the bathroom shared by the floor's residents, outside and way across the building. He thinks newspaper might work, too, like how puppies are paper-trained.

He is thankful that the dealer's boyfriend is not present, lurking around in his y-fronts. He hopes the boyfriend doesn't show up unexpectedly; he doesn't need, can't stand, the drama. Those two have a relationship that is best described as "brokeback," in that one's a needy bottom and the other's a selfish top.

The dealer pushes absent-mindedly and the head of the dildo enters him. He is trying not to flinch too much, trying not to stop the deal. The dealer is working more and more of the dildo into his hole. He can feel more shit *glacially oozing* out of his hole, or maybe it is not coming out of his hole but being stopped up by that rubber plug. His guts hurt. His heart is pounding like mad.

The dealer is still working the dildo, corkscrewing it in.

He takes a good swallow of air and his hole loosens so that the pain eases a little.

The dealer is working the dildo in and out of the ass.

He can feel even more shit coming out of the sides now. He know he is shitting. He can plainly smell it, see the earthy streaks.

The dealer doesn't seem to mind nor care, instead he is working the dildo with even brutal strokes, pushing deeper and harder, jabbing and digging as if it was a clam hunt at Pismo Beach. His face is one of concentration, single-mindedly focused on the task. The dealer lets him take another long hard hit on the pipe.

He is thankful. It helps.

Now he has stopped shitting; instead, he is bleeding. He can see the smear of blood on the thin white poly-cotton sheet. He knows it is blood because its viscosity against his bare skin is so different, unlike that of shit, or piss, or spit, or cum, or sweat, or bile, or mucus. He feels his blood flowing like his shit was flowing a moment ago.

He is surprised by how unaffected he is by all the smells in the room and the viscosity pooled under him. This is what life smells like, he thinks. Even before birth, you spend all those months in the womb shoved up beside the bowels, and then you're born mere inches away from the poophole. And when you die, your bowel is the last thing that releases its hold on your life. And in the middle, in the middle. He once, with a few friends watched a video on the internet that was reputed to be so hideously gross that it spawned millions of reaction videos of people watching the clip. "2 Girls, 1 Cup" showed two young attractive women indulging in some scat play while watched by some men. At one point in the clip, the two women crap into a plastic cup and then proceed to eat and feed the contents of the cup to each other. His friends were howling and shrieking in disbelief, one was even nauseated to the point of dry heaving. At that time, he was merely bemused by the action on screen, and all he remembered thinking was: in our lives, who among us hasn't had to eat the shit out of someone else's cup?

The dealer pulls the dildo out.

He almost passes out from the pain when the head of the dildo pops out of his ass. *How could relief feel so painful?* he might wonder, if he could even think. He is quivering, trying to quell the racking spasms. The dealer takes his forefinger and dips it into a baggie, coating his finger up to the first joint with the powder white crystals; crushed chunks and shards stick to the finger like fake snow frosting on shopping mall Christmas trees. Like coconut frosting, he thinks. The dealer puts his finger right into the open hole.

He feels his hole close on that finger like a Venus Flytrap. The finger feels strangely cold. Everything else feels magnificently hot. Soon, very soon. Everything will burn.

"Do you want a line? Here..." He takes the small packet and taps out a neat line on his belly. The sweat mats the fine powder. He gives me the McDonald's straw that has been cut into a manageable inch-and-a-half length and I sniff up what's not stuck to the sweat and the fine hairs, those I lick up, savoring the bitter taste of the powder and the salt of his sweat. I lie back down. He takes my dick and flops it onto my belly.

"Don't move," he says, and he taps out a line on the underside of my dick. The tweakered dick plumps up as he does this. He sniffs that up noisily. He takes my dick into his mouth to suck up the leftover powder. His tongue starts to go numb.

"Like Novacaine," he says.

"Like sucking spermicide," I say. I should know, and I do.

The deal was that I would collect a small vial of my cum and he would do likewise. Then we would pack it in blue-ice and FedEx it to each other. *What would you do with my cum?* he had asked. I said I would eat some of it, dribble some of it on my chest, and use some of it to jack off. And what would you do with mine? He said he would drink most of it. That's what he did with all the cum he got from all those men all over the country. But he never e-mailed me back his address and so the small bottle that once contained Body Shop Elderflower Eye Gel sat in my fridge, tightly capped and covered with aluminum foil, filled with a week-and-a-half's worth of daily (twice, thrice even) jacking off.

One day, a trick came over. A real cum pig. He wanted to drink my cum, he wanted to feel my juice on his face, dripping into his mouth. I have something better, I said. I got the bottle from the fridge. I opened the bottle and the smell of cum hit us. He was excited. I held the bottle out to him and he stuck his tongue into it. You want it? I asked. Oh yes, he begged rather all too convincingly. I let him lap at the bottle like a dog. The smell of that cum was mesmerizingly clinical, so medicinal. As he was lapping at the cum in the bottle, I noticed that a layer of mold had grown on the inside of the lid, and then I noticed a spindle of mold floating in the bottle. I held his head back, pried his mouth open with my fingers, emptied the bottle down, and shut his mouth and held it, made him swallow it all, like how you make dogs and cats take their pills.

John has put Joe in a smart pair of white y-fronts and a dog collar, and chained him to a pole. Joe's hands are bound a little too tightly and he can feel his fingers getting tingly. John is sitting in an armchair chain-smoking Camels and watching Joe. Joe is expecting something to happen. He is expecting John to give him some orders, maybe spank him, maybe some cock-and-ball torture, titclamps, clothes pegs on the nipples and scrotum, butt torture with a series of dildos, each one more menacing than the next, the dirty balled-up gym socks in his mouth as John rapes his butt; maybe John will stuff those filthy socks up his butt, or use them as a condom to fuck him. Joe's dick is getting stiff thinking of what John would do to him. But John is sitting in the armchair smoking cigarette after cigarette, staring at Joe. John doesn't look at Joe with any discernable emotion, no sense of meanness or malevolence, no desire, no disdain, no amusement, no boredom, nothing. John is not even touching himself. He is sitting there in his black jeans and green tank top smoking cigarette after cigarette. Joe thinks he can see John's eyes tearing up, but it's difficult to tell in the haze of cigarette smoke and Joe's allergies are beginning to act up, his eyes are watering, he cannot breathe easily. John is still sitting and looking at Joe, his gaze unflinching, unerring. Joe is not bored, he is not turned-on, he is not scared. He is chained to a pole, in a dog collar, in a pair of y-fronts, his hands bound a little too tight.

A few lines of good coke in the restroom at last call, then we are at his place. He sets up the rim seat in the middle of the living room. There is an alarming pile of dope carelessly and showily dumped on the coffee table. "Want to watch a video?" he asks, popping a tape into the VCR. The box is plain black and says "Russian River Weekend." The screen flickers to life and it is a scene where a hunky guy is shitting on a pudgy guy. They are in a motel room somewhere, presumably Russian River. The pudgy guys is smearing the shit all over himself as if he were icing a cake. You almost want him to start making little rosettes around the neckline.

I am seated on the rim seat, not the kind you find in medical supply stores—those are always too high—but a makeshift thing made up of a toilet seat attached to four sturdy stool legs. "Made it myself," he declares proudly. He lies on the floor and crawls under me so that his face is under my ass, and the rest of his body is sticking out from between my legs. The scene on the television has now moved on to two guys squirting their enemas out onto a third person. The third person takes the stream of brownish fluid all over his body and in his mouth. All this in the motel room somewhere in Russian River. The clean-up must be hell. I always thought a Russian River weekend would entail some river rafting, a barbecue, going for the really good fried chicken at that one restaurant, and perhaps a leisurely walk in the woods with the dogs, but obviously, I was mistaken. Or we have very different travel agents.

He starts kissing, licking, and with gusto poking at my puckered hole with his tongue. The narcotics in my bloodstream make my head torque in strange pleasurable sensations. It does what the poor choice of porn doesn't do.

Someone is in the hallway. I can see the vague shadows swaying back and forth in the dark passageway. The person is watching us from behind the stairs. "Who's that?" I ask. "Roommate?"

He replies between slobbers. "It's my mother." His iguana tongue, lick, prod, lick, suckle. I'm not sure how to react, what to say. "It's okay," he reassures me. Lick, poke, circle, lick, prod, suckle, suckle. "She has Alzheimer's, she doesn't know what happening. She's not seeing a damn thing." He continues eating my ass out, sticking his tongue as far in as he can go, lapping and slurping boisterously.

His mother sways a bit more and comes shuffling out from behind the stairs. I try to make eye contact with her. I think she sees us, I could have sworn she looked me in the eye. I'm almost certain that she smirked. But she sways and shuffles off into the kitchen in her bedroom slippers.

I can hear a familiar rustling sound coming from the kitchen. I can see his mother standing unsteadily at the kitchen counter. She has emptied the bowl of sugar packets onto the counter and is picking them up one by one, shaking them to tamp the sugar down the packet. With great difficulty, she tears open the packet and with shaky hands, she pours the contents of the packet into her mouth. A good portion of the sugar misses her open, gaping, wound-like mouth and sprinkles the front of her gray housedress, printed with little apples and oranges, with white crystals that sparkle in the yellow lights of the gas cooker. She takes another packet, shakes it, tears it open, and pours the sugar into her mouth, or tries as best as her deteriorating motor skills allow, dusting her dress with more sparkle. And another packet. And another. More sugar. I can hear her crunching the sugar; I can hear her grinding the crystals between the molars of her dentures. Soon there is a pile of empty sugar packets on the kitchen counter. The front of her housedress is dusted with so many sugar crystals that it looks as if it is a frumpy sequined gown made for some low-rent suburban drag queen.

He is working his fingers into my arsehole. All his tonguing and licking has worked my hole and loosened the sphincter. Unplanned encounters do not facilitate adequate cleaning or preparation. And with all the prying of fingers and tongues, I feel myself lose control and a small splat of soft shit falls out onto his face. But he opens his mouth wide, and catches most of it. The smell of my own shit repulses me. I am embarrassed. I don't want to carry on. I want to get up and wipe up, clean off, go home. But he's still licking and sucking and cleaning my murky hole. I force myself to cum, and the effort of that makes me shit more onto his face, and he eats that up, too. With his shit-streaked hands, he grabs his dick and in a few quick short pumps, disposes of his load. His face is still in my ass, he is whimpering like a puppy, still licking at my ass.

I get up from the chair, ignoring the dribble down my leg, and walk over to the coffee table and selfishly scrape together the biggest fattest line I think I can handle and force it up my nose, the bits that I cannot hold in there, which fall out of my nostrils back onto the glass plate, I wipe up with my finger and swab onto my gums. I think I am going to black out. I'm not sure how I'm going to get home, and I definitely don't want to stay here, though I might not have a choice. He is still lying on the floor with a satiated cheesy grin on his face. His mother is standing there in the dim-lit kitchen eating sugar, the sandpapery rasp and crunch between her false teeth, staring into space, trapped in her own brain, staring at us. At the very end. At the forking road. At the closing gyre. You will know what you are. You may even know who. And even if it is just for the briefest of a flicker, taken on some rare forgiving shameless night or day, you will see all the exit signs, all the detours and off-ramps, all flashing lights lit up just for you.

Woo

1.

My suitor is a jack-booted thug, a gangster who stomped on my heart as if it were the liver of a swarthy nemesis. I lie in bed at night wondering who he is bullying and what he is doing with his pale hollow friends, for he never works alone. Not even when he is beside me, even inside me; he is never alone, he comes with far too many people.

I lie in bed and he appears by my window like the Blue Angel. My one confidant thinks the appearance is more like Jiminy Cricket. In the cartoon, the popular version: the conscience that lives in the wooden doll's head, ready to chastise and to prod awake the mechanisms of guilt. In the original version, smashed to bits in the second chapter, squished under the boot of the evil wooden doll: a bug, a pest, nothing more.

My suitor takes me by the hand and leads me down mad corridors and unfamiliar avenues. It is as if we were flying (but I have a fear of flying, of heights, of crashing, of flight, of speed, of air, altogether too many fears), and we land on a grassy lawn speckled with flecks of motor oil and engine grease. He takes me by the hand and he shows me a gorgeous building that he will burn down to cinders to prove his love for me. The beautiful marbled tiles, the intricate wooden panels, the luxurious carpeting, all mean nothing to him: these objects of crafted beauty are merely cotton and wool saturated with kerosene in his sore eyes. He places a matchstick in my hand, and guiding my small fist, strikes it against the side of a matchbox to watch it crackle into its horrible flame. Then he takes me by the elbow and leads me in a tango, a foxtrot, to the side of the building, the single flair of light the only illumination in the dark night. Hand in hand in lit match, we touch the side of the building with the tenderness of a vetrinarian, and he brings everyone inside of him to me.

I lie in bed and he appears at my window like Jiminy Cricket. I try to smash him with my boot, then my sneakers, but to no avail, his abdomen doesn't split open and spill its green guts like bugs would as he is not made of exoskeleton as insects are, but of real bone holding his flesh and helping his blood along the mad twisting paths of his fury.

I do not subscribe to any of his infuriating doctrines and silly conspiracies, and I tell him that he is nothing to think such thoughts; and still he comes to my window in a deranged state. I tell him he is mad to act on his cancer, and still he shows up at my window as regular as heartache and Hallmark holidays. I tell myself that I am insane, total batshit, and am slowly slipping into a raving pit the size of the Antarctic peopled by every demon known to Bible folk, but still I fly even as I fear flight. I fight even as I fear pain and conflict. I fly with him, follow his crusades across a terrain of tedium that holds nothing true for me.

I lie in bed and wait for someone to save me. Many show up but then they are just the people inside of him. A trick of light and night. And again, I'm flying and I'm fearing and I wish for the chartered seaplane, the magic carpet, the spread span of wings to fail and let us crash so hard to the earth, smash into the smallest roots of the tallest tree, and there we shall stay, there we shall make a little home away from the cranking madness of it all.

2.

So many lovers diseased and maimed. I have seen everyone of them somewhere before, a bright red despair in my guts. The sounds always sound better with the moon full of cancer, and white beasts crawl across the unanswerable extent of my urges: the one I chose was the one with the white eyelids that peeled off. That was the due, the dotted line above his eyeball and the tiny lifting flaps that facilitated such an easy peel.

And should I choose wrongly, should I choose at all from among this bunch of rejects, castoffs: the young one with skin so saggy, his face lifts off like a rubber mask. The one with nipples ingrown to dank pits in his chest cavity, the ribs parted to let the rot sink in. The hayseed one with fingers and toes, pieces of nose, a whole ear, fallen off in a year's worth of leprous fits. The old one with gangrenous opals for eyes, asbestos pipes for hands, and chipped new age crystals for a cock. Should I choose what I chose, I chose?

He was the only one in the running. I was only running. My pick would have such white eyelids that flutter and fall off like the last petals on the last white flower at an outdoor wake; I chose a funeral in a bitter storm. What was left behind after the wilting and falling were the bitterest eyes. *Like a corpse*, my dear soon-to-be late father said, *just like a corpse.*

My siblings tell me stories about how certain unfortunate folk meet their ends with their eyes open: fiery deaths in closed spaces, rat poison suicides, hypothermia, certain blood fevers borne by biting insects no smaller than the period which ends all our louched sentences. I join in to remind them: Jeanne D'Arc met her glorious end with her eyes wide open in rapturous quiver; and so did our Christ, in some stories and certain version of the Gospel, where it is said that our Christ, in passion on the cross, faced the loss of His Father with eyes open, looking straight through the gates of Hell and beyond, all the way through into his boudoir in the Kingdom of Heaven.

In school, we had to dissect rats. Mangy things with wet fur, their original white turned so muddy with sewer goop that they elicited no ounce of pity, even as their filthy rat-lungs squeaked and collapsed, as we pushed large pins into their crunchy paws, impaling them onto a tray of wax, preparing to slice through from neck to anus. No pity even as we grew up, weaned on cute singing mice and heroic rats in cartoons and animated movies, rodents intelligent enough to outwit cats and dogs and humans. The dissection lesson went routinely except for one incident. A young classmate, upon cutting into her assigned rat, found that the rat was cancerous; the stink emanating from the decayed insides of the rodent caused the student to scream out in sheer disgust, disrupting the class. Upon assignment of another rodent, the student dutifully cut into the animal only to be assailed with that familiar stench and the familiar sight of green-blackened guts. Two more rats were dug out of their cages, chloroformed, and assigned, but both were cancerous, too. Both reeking of that same foul stench that was judiciously taking over the classroom. An air freshener, supposedly Spring Linen, was employed to fight the whiffs of decay. By this time, the teacher was losing patience and ordered that the next rat was to be the last one assigned. Sobbing and shaking, the student held her scalpel and nervously brought the sharp edge to the final rat's flesh. The surgical-precise blade only had to prick the second dermis of the rat, and that stench, now so familiar to all in the classroom, seeped out of the rat. Cancerous, again; but determined to maintain discipline and order, the teacher ordered the student to proceed; and sobbing and shivering even more, the student pushed on, picking out the necessary organs and stretching them out on the wax tray, sketching them in her workbook, documenting their color, texture, and what was partially digested in its rotting intestines.

Later in the semester I saw that student's workbook and the sketches of the cancered guts were the most beautiful things I had ever seen. I do not know whether that was testament to her artistic genius or if it was really what was found in the insides of that cursed fifth rodent. It was as if the slicing into the low, and lower still, in disease and rot; there, in the leak of failed organs and foul blood and stink, there in the face of a corpse or a suitor without eyelids, his holes perpetually pus-infected, one might witness a vision where angels of every order kiss one another secretly to their God's displeasure.

3.

I came into the charms of this husband by way of the fantastic promises he whispered into my ear and my arse-crack when I was a mere innocent teenage virgin.

I now hate his flaky peeling lips and the smell of his gums, but what choice do I have; poor poor pitiful me, forced to live with my equally poor poor pitiful sibling, my parasitic twin, attached to my coccyx, barely alive and breathing shallow like salamanders. I keep my twin hidden in the folds of my clothes; a task especially hard in the summer when everyone is wearing capri pants and espadrilles; there is nothing fashionable, off-the-racks that can properly hide a parasitic twin.

But this was my destiny, fate, if you believe that sort of thing. At that tender age, I was rendered despondent, depressed by way of terrifying nightmares. In the dream, I saw a land of trees and greenery burning in flames, airplanes dashed overhead spewing orange plumes, the trees shrivel, and the landscape turns an unflinching sausage-brown. In the brown streets unshaded by these wilted bunch of branch and twigs, all manner of beast and child, naked, with open sores, pus and fluids running down their twig-thin bodies, third degree burns blistering and untreated, run like Olympic racers but with no sense of direction, nowhere to go. In one version of the dream, there is a diminishing jungle, the type seen only in movies, recreated in Hollywood back lots or on golf courses in the Third World; the jungle is chock full of animals though all of them are oddly silent; all their larynges have been severed; even the crickets and the cicadas do not make a sound, their legs amputated. The only sound is a pitiful whining and yelping, and the high-pitched whine gets louder and shriller and fades away and returns all year around, unceasingly; and the animals and insects sit where they are, transfixed by this sound which goes on for years; and no one moves for years.

That was my recurring nightmare, my regression. My parents employed specialists and nurses, psychologists and mystics to lure a life out of me. They tried bribes of sweets and cash, threats of beatings, but nothing worked, the world of my nightmares stained its indelible scrawl in my immature mind, leached in, spread too vast, too hooked to draw its talons out. The parents threw their hands up in defeat. *Let the little bastard be*, they eventually declared.

It was then I met the soon-to-be husband. He was a visiting houseguest, newly emergent in his time. His breath smelled of tarnished metal even then.

One accidental whiff of that metallic burr of his mouth and I wanted to vomit but my stomach was empty, and still somehow, his funny loose ways flexed me, and I was finally bespoke in my still clasped clench.

From then on, I saved my newly pupated life for the suitor-to-be-husband who waited as patiently as he did. Weather permitting, when the grass was cut, we lay on the damp ground, looking at clouds and all manner of flies; I enjoyed rolling around the lawn like a hedgehog. It was in this state that I thought I might conceivably love him in some manageable way.

When I was years older, I imagined every excruciating detail about my shadow life ending. I crawled into my head and saw such simple uncomplicated dreams in all their crossed-haired wires, and so, nothing more. But that tarnished metal smell shocked me as smelling salts would, jerking me back to ground zero zero point zero one.

On that last night, did he, metallic gums and all, mumble, *there will still be time for salvage.* (At least that was what I thought I heard.) And like a dream, I the somnambulist slowly climbed each rung of deep sleep, rung until the end of days.

Sleep-paste worn off my eyes, I jumped back into my life; the husband was gone, left for another, a younger more innocent one. And my awful sibling twin, silent when I was, and still silent when I was not, did indeed die soon after. She breathed her last sighing breath and drooped from my tailbone, never to be missed, never to be answered to.

4.

I saw heretics at a wedding: great ugly behemoths casting a rain of rice and brimstone on the unfortunate couple.

The groom in tails and tie, carnation in buttonhole, dashes down the aisle with his bride, a mob of white lace flying behind, a super-hero's cape if that's what heroes are reduced to these days. The rice grains burn as harsh as acid rain, scorch the guests and the minister, but the happy couple, protected by their unyieldingly sure devotion, were unharmed. The rings exchanged were ancient finger traps designed to amputate clean below the knuckle; the minister was a pederast fucking the flower girls and the pageboys behind a tapestry of the Virgin Mother receiving her immaculate conception, her cunt juices flowing so freely in rivulets down her legs, stray dogs would lap it up and pigeons would bathe in it, devotees collect the ichthyic fluid in goblets and in thimbles, and make communion from it. At the reception, the cake was spiked with ground glass; the punch was poisoned with latex emulsifiers; the salmon finger sandwiches harbored salmonella and bread mold.

I saw heretics at a wedding kissing the bride and groom with the familiarity of a sea bass, a proud clown hired for a birthday party. The hookers and their pimps sashay down the street and leer; the bookie counts his wad and jots witticisms he overhears at the race track down in the little black book he keeps taped to his inner thigh; the panhandler paints himself red and writes manifestos about the rise of communism, claiming with Baptist fervor prophesying that the hole-in-the-wreck bar down in skid row will be the site of the revolution which will wipe the world clean of its vile greed and potato recipes, and every weekend will be May Day and the children will be let out of school early so they can wash their state-approved pets and learn about the institutions, like marriage, that they will have to participate in eventually.

The happy couple kiss under the banner of god and family and love; they will fornicate when appropriate, they will create litter upon litter of newborns, all with sharp teeth and bawling dispositions; each litter of carbon-copies even genetic engineering couldn't have created any better who long for mothers and fathers and milk and money and meat. This, this cycle, is multiplied over and over, unquestioned; and the heretics for centuries to come will never be unemployed, nor want for any entertainment, nor any passion.

This was what I saw.

Marriages

1.

My husband came home with The Clap. Actually, it was more of a standing ovation. His job in insurance has him traveling around the state to all sorts of podunk towns. It's shameful that the public restrooms in so many of these places aren't maintained to proper sanitary standards. The Surgeon General really ought to speak out about this issue. Use the toilet tissue to make a seat cover protector or use newspaper, I tell him, or squat on the bowl. But he never listens. On the positive side, the penicillin shots should help clear up the acne on his back.

2.

My husband and I have absolutely no qualms about public displays of affection. We often stroll down the street hand-in-hand, or arm-in-arm, gazing contentedly into each others' eyes, not caring about who stares or gawks. When the mood strikes us, we might even embrace and kiss each other deeply and intensely. We're not ashamed of our love. And if they don't notice us at first, we double back and stand directly in front of them and kiss and make out and fondle each other, in a tasteful manner, of course. We believe it is important for others to see what perfect love looks like.

3.

When I got home, I discovered that my husband was possessed by an evil spirit, a horrible demon. I called the only exorcist that was listed in the Yellow Pages, but the earliest he could come was in two days. What could we do? We had no choice but to wait and tough it out.

My demon-possessed husband yelled and screamed at me, calling me all sorts of hateful and mean names. Then he started smacking me around and throwing things at my head. He played twinkie porn loudly on all the television sets. He forced me to perform various vile and depraved sex acts but when I tried to kiss him, he would turn away with a repulsed look. He started calling his penis Neil, and his left testicle, Nigel. His right testicle refused to participate; Good for you, right testicle, I say. He, Nigel, and Neil would gossip viciously about me as if I wasn't in the room. I'd walk into a room and find them huddled together whispering and sniggering and when they see me, they start giggling insanely and then I'd hear Nigel cackling from another room. How do they do that? The devil surely works in mysterious way among men.

Actually, this was exactly just like it was in our regular life, except that he wasn't trying to humiliate or belittle me in public or in front of our friends.

When the exorcist came to our door, I told him we did not need his help after all, the demon had left and we were okay.

4.

My husband's mother in a bid to improve herself has enrolled at the barely accredited College of Cosmetology and Cosmetic Surgery. They're not the same thing, you know that right? I tell my husband.

Well, duh, he says, obviously. Otherwise it'd be called the College of Cosmetology *or* Cosmetic Surgery.

To show his support, he has offered to be her final graduating project. You're not plain, I tell him. But he's doing something to his face with a blackhead remover that is simultaneously fascinating and repulsive, and not listening to me. He's ready for beauty.

And now, he can hardly sit because of the silicone butt injections. The dark circles of his raccoon eyes belie the chemical peel, and peek from behind the bandages covering his face. Strangers, handsome men on the street, keep running up to him to give him their phone numbers or business cards, they give him obscene propositions scribbled on the backs of receipts and any old scrap of paper or napkin; they're so sure that there's a Clooney-esque hunk underneath all that bandage and surgical tape.

I'm hoping that she fails. Or gets a C-. Or takes an incomplete. I'm not choosy.

5.

How did I go from being the most irresistible person in the world to becoming the most irritating person in the world? How long did that change, that metamorphosis, take to occur? Was there a pupating stage? And was I anyone else in the process? Most agreeable? Most nonchalant? Most oblivious? Most forgiving? Most wtf?

Obviously I did not see the changes happening. So were they seamless transitions? Or were there definite beginning and ending points, starts and stops, as if we were driving a stick shift for the first time. Was it all plain for everyone to see? Or could only one person see this happening?

Why won't anyone tell me? The only person who knows all the answers is my husband, but he's still not home. I'm calling his cellphone again. I've text-messaged him repeatedly and left countless voicemail messages but I still haven't heard back one squeak from him.

6.

After dinner, while I was doing the dishes, my husband fished out $40 from my wallet and said he was going to the corner store to buy some cigarettes, a carton of milk, a bag of potato chips, Diet Coke, and some lottery scratchers. I like the Lightly Salted variety, I called out after him as he left the house.

When he finally returned home ten days later, smoking his cigarette as he sauntered through the front door with a carton of rancid milk in his hand, I ask, what happened with the chips? He finished the chips on the way home, he said, he was sorry. And the scratchers? They didn't have the kind he liked, and besides, he scratched them all and every one was a dud. And the Diet Coke? He forgot that.

It's not that he's selfish or thoughtless, it's that he sometimes just doesn't think things through is all.

7.

My husband snores as if it's the end of the world. We have a mid-sized studio apartment and I'm often cranky for lack of a good night's sleep.

Try sleeping on your back, friends suggest. Or sleeping with a tennis ball taped to your side. Or a golf ball. Try elevating your feet, or your hips. Try wearing thick socks on one foot. How about a nose clip? A hairclip on the right side? The left side? Try drinking some brandy before bed. Hot milk? Olive oil and apple slices? For me, they suggest, tug on his pillow. Elbow him sharply. Friends offer all sorts of advice but nothing works. Every night when we go to bed it's as if a garbage truck is fighting with a hippopotamus right there in the room. Try a white-noise machine, someone suggests. But that just ended up with me trying to sleep on a beach while a garbage truck is fighting a hippopotamus as seagulls attack them both.

So when he had a heart attack and had to be warded in the hospital, I was delighted. Finally! Finally I could get a good night's sleep or two. But I could not.

Now when he snores, I turn my back to him and press up close to him, back to back, so I can feel the vibrating timbre. The buzzing reassures me that he's not dead in bed beside me. I stick a pillow over my head and I slowly drift off. I am in the Serengeti and we are sitting in lawn chairs amidst the tall grasses, the sun is about to set, and we each have a small tumbler of black coffee in hand. I look not unlike Isak Dinesen, before the syphilis turned her into a shriveled little monkey, of course. My husband reaches over and holds my hand as the sun dips below the horizon. In the distance, a garbage truck is fighting with a couple of hippopotamuses. Oh look! A puma and a lion stalking in the grass are about to pounce into the melee. What? The seagulls and a couple of buzzards and a pelican want to join in, too? Sure, why not. Here comes an ape with a spanner in one hand and a wind chime in the other jumping into the mess. This is going to go on for a while.

I'm rooting for the ape. I affectionately call him Preparation Ape. The only person who would find that amusing is my husband. And on cue, I hear him guffaw, then the snoring resumes.

8.

Those three little words rear their icky hydra heads. No, not "Here's some cash!" though that's quite good, too. The other three words that mean everything and nothing, which encompasses the constellation to a wad of phlegm at the bottom of your lung, which spins the axis of living things but is powerless to stop a door closing, which is unspeakable yet uttered every 2.3 seconds by someone somewhere in the world in whatever language, some might even mean what they say, but mostly it's a matter of what the other hears. You will succumb to it; everyone does once at least, eventually. You may triumph over it, or think you do, or you might let it ruin you, turn you into fungus.

Oops. It's 2 seconds, 2 point 1, 2 point 2, do you hear someone saying it?

Someone says, "I love you."

Someone else says, "Okay. Define *Love*."

"I love you, too, but I'm married."

"You don't love me, you just think that you do because I represent the freedom that you desire in your cloistered life."

2 seconds, 2 point 1, 2 point 2, someone else says:

"I'm sorry, couldn't quite hear you. What was that again?"

"Let's be friends!"

"Stop, don't spoil what we have together by saying that."

"Who are you? Stop following me or I'll call the police."

2 seconds, 2 point 1, 2 point 2, someone else says:

"No. You lust me. But that's okay."

"Love is an artificial construct but it's not your fault that you've been oppressed, brainwashed even, by our late Capitalist culture. Hey, can I get a backrub?"

2 seconds, 2 point 1, 2 point 2, someone else says:

"But the Winter Olympic pairs figure skating tryouts are in

three weeks, we have to focus. This is not the right time."

"I can only love Jesus Christ, my personal lord and savior. Do you know that He died for you? So you could have eternal life? Do you?"

"You amuse me! You say the most outrageous things."

2 seconds, 2 point 1, 2 point 2, someone else says:

"Shut up! My pimp will hear you! He hates anyone saying that."

2 seconds, 2 point 1, 2 point 2. Or perhaps someone else says:

Thank you for telling me that. And I want you to know that I mean every single thing I'm telling you now, even as I can't look you in the eye – here, let me lean my head against you to slow down this cyclone all around me. I think that you are a spectacular and amazing person and I like you very very much and I think I might even love you or be able to fall in love with you. But I haven't been in that state of being for such a long time, and past experiences have gnawed and beaten me up so much that I'm not sure I even know what that state feels like anymore, or that I would recognize it even if it crawled up my leg and bit me on the inside of my arse. So I ask that you be patient with me. Be patient with me and forgive me. Forgive me, for I am an incomplete idiot even at the best of times and circumstances. Forgive me, for I will cling to illogicalities, I will wear down the hooks and hooves of my insecurities on your back. My timing will be arrhythmic and as dependable as a fake Seiko under water, as precise as a cockeyed raccoon ballet. Forgive me because I know I will inevitably hurt your feelings while not even being aware that I'm doing it. I will be defensive and unthinking and lash out to protect all that is void or nonexistent or useless. So forgive me ever more and be ever more patient with me. And when the time comes, should I not be in love with you, then I'm a complete fool who doesn't deserve yours or anyone else's love, for who could not love someone with such qualities of patience and forgiveness and open-heartedness? Now hold me tight as I lean closer into you, tighter still, because I have this incredible and uncontrollable urge to simply and quietly cry as I lean into you and remind myself what you smell like, as I remember what home smells like.

First

There is a proper name for everything that exists in this world. The groove in corduroy. The piece of green paper in take-away sushi packs, cut to look like grass that separates the wet ginger from the moisture-hungry seaweed. The bulging nodes at the base of Morning Glory stems that bend when touched. The blue fluid inside ice-packs. That small dot behind the eye of the clownfish.

There is a name for all ephemeral things, too. Emotions, thoughts, processes, all named by scientists, poets, novelists, dictionary compilers, university professors, journalists, and celebrities, all recorded and stored in the Library of Congress, the Patent and Trademark Offices, local libraries, in endless files stacked up in nameless offices and museums basements around the world.

The sound of Velcro coming apart. The red-tinted ghosts with long oily hair that haunt rubber plantations in Malaysia. The sexual fetish of being aroused by having your genitals touched with barbecue tongs. The different stages of rigor mortis. The bacteria that hangs in the San Francisco air which causes sourdough to turn so. The particular sort of blistering that crack smoke burns in the soft tissue of the throat. The gradients of sweat and their odors.

Then there are the phobias. Each dutifully studied, catalogued, and named by a psychologist with the care of a father naming a first-born. The fear of horseradish. The fear of brown paper bags. The fear of plastic products, velour, wooden chopsticks. Even something as specific as the paralyzing fear of *Sesame Street* characters has a name. I'm being serious. I once knew a woman who, as a young innocent college intern, worked at the studio where one of the many versions of that venerable children's show was produced. The man inside of Big Bird would strut around in his yellow-feathered costume, without the head and beak, of course, and sexually harass her, making lewd comments and touching her inappropriately with his big yellow-feathered wings. This went on for weeks, she said, but she really wanted the job and was young, confused, and scared, and did not know what to do. Eventually, the men whose hands were shoved up all day inside fluffy furry Ernie, Bert, and Oscar the Grouch started to pull their hands out of their Muppets and desired to put them inside the woolly sweaters she wore, as was the fashion at the time. It was as if they had this *thing* for fuzzy fabric, she said. One day while channel-surfing, she accidentally clicked on NBC's *Muppets On Ice* special. The sight of Big Bird and the whole motley crew on ice skates doings loops and salchows made her scream uncontrollably; she had a nervous breakdown and had to be institutionalized. To this day, the mere suggestion of those Muppets makes her break into a panic attack.

There is a name for everything that exists, which no longer exists, or will soon cease to exist. Whether you know its proper name is another matter altogether.

Adam is dreaming. What can the first person on the planet possibly be dreaming about? What could be lurking in his mind given the vast expanse of unnamed terrain that lies before him: a colossal ice desert, an equally eternal sand desert, immeasurable forests, the acrid savannah teaming with insects, rainforest upon rainforest filled with flora and fauna, beasties and buggies. Time he knows of. Seven days to be exact and many more of this cycle will follow. Until weeks turn to endless years. But apart from that, he has no memory, no history; he was born an adult, slapped together with primeval mud and the snot of God.

The only clues we may have in understanding his experiences are those of amnesia victims and Donald Duck.

Amnesia victims are the easy one. Car crash, severe shock, visitations by evil spirits, and some folks' minds are blasted into a state of chaos, their neurons and synaptic switches become as tangled as a phone cord and suddenly, they forget everything prior to a stated moment. Some manage to get jarred into recovery; others wander through life and eventually recover their memories in bits and pieces. Some become another person completely, a person born an adult with no past and no lived references. The only remnants of this past lived life are a language that the person has no idea how he learned or even how eloquent or mumbly he ever used it, and mementos, lots of them, which their past gleefully foists on them. But in vain: the teddy bear with the punched-in nose has no sentimental value anymore. A once cherished wedding ring reeks with crassness. Photo albums become useless burdens and gather dust on the top shelves. The record collection does not trigger any memories, fond or foul.

Forced to live within the locus of their bodies, the amnesia victims are nothing but humans wrecked on a seashore of foundless memories, fogged in by their billion imploded brain cells. They will recollect or recreate.

On the other hand, Donald Duck, the hot-tempered, lovably

mischievous but well-intentioned character that Disney created to shadow Mickey's bland niceness and squeaky clean-cut values, lives beyond his plump feathered body. He has traveled to the center of the earth, beyond Neptune and Pluto, to mythical lands of legends and lore, to every continent in great adventures, and still he has no memory of his travels, his experiences, the people he met, the creatures he fought, the exotic food he greedily scoffed down, or the pleasures of which he partook. In some narratives, he's foolish, the dunce, unable to remember facts accurately; in another, he's a mechanical genius; in yet another, the rugged outdoorsman. The only constants in his life are his nephews, his miserly Uncle Scrooge, and his passion for Daisy Duck. And even then, their own mental states are somewhat in question, too.

In a parody postcard that can be found in gift shops, Donald is sitting on a green stool, the yellow stripe on the right sleeve of his trusty sailor suit tightened into a tourniquet as Donald devilishly grips a hypodermic needle in his left hand and shoots up. His eyes, blotted out by a black strip, belie a fiendish squint. Donald, unable to remember any of his experiences, will never be able to remember this high, he will not know the comforting warm sting of fluid pumping into his vein. He will not know the unplumbed horrors of coming down or withdrawal. Or the agony of the infection gurgling in that awful festering abscess on his forearm, his veins bruised and collapsed. His addiction will never exacerbate nor will it ever abate, qualities quite uncommon for an addict.

Adam is leaning against a tree sleeping and he is dreaming. His lost rib, the gargantuan task of naming all other living creatures, plagues his mind, we can surmise. But how will these stresses manifest themselves in Adam's subconscious? There is no way that he can know what to make of his dream-life, or even his waking life. Nothing has yet been named, he cannot lift his hand to his mouth and call it suppressing a yawn. He cannot scratch his groin and call it itchy. He cannot piss and shake his penis in relief. All these he can do, but he will have no context as to how or why or what he is doing and why he has done it or how it should feel.

Adam's task is indeed colossal. Even with the historic breath of language, grammar, and colloquialism, we still have problems naming certain things for sure. Even something as simple and as everyday as a city. What is a city? Is it an incorporated municipality within defined boundaries with legal powers established in a charter? Some could define a city simply as a town of significant size. The academics will think of something undecipherable and frightfully tedious. The humanists would probably define a city by its inhabitants.

Hmmmm. Imagine a city where the inhabitants do not know where they are; perhaps they have all been hypnotized by carnies at the turnpike or more likely have all been drunk driving in an alcoholic black-out. They wake up/sober up/regain consciousness to find themselves in this particular place and have decided to stay here. Why not? There is ample cheap housing, the cost of living is peanuts, and moreover, there are extended Happy Hours and a Velcro Human Fly game in all of the city's 642 bars and 2324 mini-bars.

What a city this will be: filled with the alcoholic surly, the alcoholic pathological, the alcoholic happy, and the recovering alcoholic. The word 'bi-polar' would have been invented here, if Adam had not already done his job. The industries that will emerge from this city, and come to characterize it, would be 12-Step Support Groups, Self-Help Psychobabble, Psychotherapy, and Gastroenterology, in both their traditional and holistic forms. This would also be the place where the concept of the Super-Bar, the Mega-Bar, and the Hyper-Bar was conceived over an early draft of the mojito (had chicory, too many mint twigs, but you could see where it was headed). Each of these bar types differed from the next by the number of imported beers served, the shape and volume of the beer mugs, the ratio of video games and pool tables to the height of the chairs, and of course, by the available merchandising. Only Hyper-Bars are licensed to make lobster-flavored saltine crackers emblazoned with the establishment's name. Clam dip was always optional.

And if I woke and found myself here, what would I do? How will I live here? Can I even? I'm such a lightweight drinker; but then I have contexts, notions, ideas to help tool me along. I might manage.

"How's it going, Adam man!" It's been Happy Hour for more than an hour, and Adam has finally staggered in, looking quite ratty. His tie and his breast pocket are stained with ink that is leaking from his ballpoint pen. Just last week, I helped him name Pocket Protector, but he just doesn't get it. His hair is a mess (we had helped him name Wedge Cut last year), and his eyes are ringed with big dark circles. (Charmaine, the bar wench, helped him name Clinique Ultra-Hydroxy Moisturizing Eye Gel. Non-comedogenic will be named next week, and we shall all be thankful.)

"I need something, something double," he groans. The bartender takes pity and pours him a triple Jack Daniels, which confuses Adam, but he drinks it nonetheless. Adam named Double years and years ago, but the whole idea of relativity still hasn't sunk in yet. He's a little hung up on weights and measures, and he should be, that one project took years to finish, and only with a huge grant from the Sung Dynasty who were trying to push it so that they could get along with that damn silk trade: huge bins of silk worms twitching their little silken asses off into silky spindles were dawdling in bins all across the Canton harbor, and the Arabs were getting antsy for new fabrics for their new line of harem pants.

We're all drinking margaritas because it is Happy Hour and the margarita is a happy drink. The secret ingredient is Triple Sec, which hasn't been officially named yet, but it'll be easy to slip that one in later.

Adam starts, "I'm so glad evolution has slowed down, I only have fifteen animal species left to name. Then there's all these frogs in Mendocino that have been growing new limbs or less limbs and some of them have been growing more eyes and turning into some other thing altogether. Maybe in a few more years they'll turn to birds. It's screwing up my filing system. The work was piling up and I sent a memo to God for help, and so he got rid of a few species. Extinction, it's my Labor Day present from the big guy.

"And that's just the animals. I have all these other stuff to name, too. This week alone, I had to name five new cheeses. Why don't those goddamn Dutch just stop it already? It's hard to name cheese, you should try it sometime. Do it wrong and Kraft calls you up to bitch about how they can't sell it by such a sissy name. Gruyere was a lovely name, I thought."

"Here, you need to try this Velcro Human Bar Fly game," I tell him, leading him to the section of the bar set up for this very amusement, and helping him into the Velcro suit.

"What's this pokey stuff?" Adam asks.

"Velcro," I tell him.

"Velcro? Who named that? I didn't name this stuff. I hadn't even gotten to it yet."

"Hey, things get named, we all just can't wait for you to get around to it, can we?" I tell him as I shoot him from the launcher. Adam flies through the air and smashes into the Velcro wall target, groin right smack in the red spot of the bull's-eye.

"Ow," he whines, "this is fucked. This is definitely fucked." And the midget that always trails Adam with a notepad and a laptop computer duly notes 'Fucked.'

"Next week, they're getting the inflatable sumo wrestling game! It's a flesh-colored suit you put on and they fill it up with air so that you're big and puffy like a sumo wrestler and then you smash into each other until someone vomits," the lush at the end of the bar who looks not unlike Faye Dunaway in *Barfly* tells us.

"Ah, sumo. That was one of my easiest ones to name. The Japanese ones were so easy!" Adam sighs, "Why can't they all be like that. I am just not naming any more things in French. Or Korean."

"So, Adam, I want to ask you for a favor," I say. "Can you put something on the fast track?"

"Oh shit, it's not some new beast or cheese, is it?"

"No, no, nothing of that sort. Well, you see, there's this guy..."

"Ah! Lover. Boyfriend. Significant other. Friend. Date. Husband, diminutive: hubby. Old-man. Other half. Master. Mister. Beau. Best mate. Best man. Fiancé. Soul mate," Adam rattles off.

"Nothing like that, nothing so formed. It's something that's just in the initial bits," I say.

"We have names for that kind of stuff!" Adam beams. "Swain. Inamorata. Adorer. Amorist. Infatuate. Paramour. Suitor, Wooer. Pursuer. Flame. Casanova. Romeo. Don Juan." The midget taps Adam on the knee, Adam leans down, and the midget whispers in his ear and shows him the computer screen. "Oh yes, Idol. Jewel. Pet. Cherished. Crush. Any of those work so far?"

"Well, no, it's...."

"Aha! No problemo!" Adam exclaims, "I have just the thing! Sweetheart. Honey. Snuggle bunny. Pookie, variation: Pookie-bear. Snookums, variation: Snookie. Woo-woo. Puppy, variation: Puppy-pooh. Pooh-bear. Feel free to offer variations such as Honey-Pookie-Snuggle-Bunny, or Snookie-Pookie, or Pookie-Woo-Woo. I don't quite care for the woo-woo thing myself, but it's quite common and popular in Australia, I'm told."

"I wish I could use those," I sigh. "But the circumstances are a little more hazy. I don't know where this whole thing is heading. I think of him constantly, and he possesses my every waking thought. I even called the radio psychic to find out my destiny."

"Ah, I remember that day we did 'Destiny,' good day that was, an inspired day that was," Adam reminisces. "Then that Destiny's Child shows up and makes it all soppy, screws it all up for everyone."

"They were better as a four-piece, better harmonies, rounder sound," the midget chimes in. And he's totally correct, too.

"Sally the Psychic said it would work out, but it hasn't. Why would she give me faulty advice on an Arbitron-rated Best for Easy Listening Lite Rock station, the radio station that everyone at work can agree on? I'm hopelessly smitten by this guy. I have detailed fantasies about us: it started quite simply, romantic vacations, camping trips, matching tattoos, a night at the opera, but last night I found myself dreaming about us in *Supermarket Sweep*. He was running down the aisles with the wobbly shopping cart under perfect control in his gorgeous tattooed arms, and I was screaming product names at him. Lysol Linen-Fresh Disinfectant, Ray-O-Vac 12-Pak, Deep Woods Off!, Tide with Bleach, Springfield Chicken Chunk Pot-Pies, Snicker's, for god's sake, Snicker's. I don't even use half of those things and I don't know whether he does or not. I long to hear his voice, even over the static of the phone line, but he has call forwarding so I can't even call to hear his voice on the answering machine message. I hunt for his name on the Internet everyday and bookmark every instance of it. I look at his name in the phonebook just to pass the time. I hide behind parked cars and municipal trash bins so that I can just look at him."

"I think you're looking for Stalker or Obsessed or Unrealistically romantic or Romantique, if you please," Adam says.

"And every time I see him, every time I watch him move, I think I feel some crusty cosmic fingernail poking at my very insides. I have no word for what I'm going through. I don't know what I am, he is, or how to sleep or wake. I need a word for this condition that I've found myself in."

Adam looks flummoxed. He looks defeated. "Wow, that *is* a difficult one. If only because the condition is imaginary, unrealistic, too idealized, and that, my dear friend, can be called by any name and it would still make no difference or sense."

The midget shaking his head slowly in resignation has tucked his notebook away and has powered his laptop off.

Happiness is not the remedy for unhappiness.

Oops.

happiness is not the remedy for unhappiness.

King

When the dumping occurs, friends rally around. They look doleful in solidarity, they tread lightly, they offer sentimental platitudes intended to uplift, to raise hope, to soothe. *Better to have lost in love, then never...*, they say, *You deserve better...*, they declare, *It's his loss..., It was never meant to be...*

Yes, there are plenty of fish in the sea. But there is also jellyfish and mercury poisoning. Go fish.

The guy I was dating sent me an e-mail telling me that his life was too busy to have to factor me into the equation of work and school and family and friends and obligations. We can still hang out, he writes. The e-mail contained an attachment, an unwieldy ten megabyte image file which I think is a picture of him, but it's all pixilated into swirly bits of a million and two colors, as if the Shiseido make-up counter exploded in his face. Apparently someone still had time to break in his new bong and play with Photoshop for eight hours.

It's as if the very last dinosaur or the last mammoth – or in my case, the very last dodo bird – suddenly looked up and realized that evolution had kicked in. Something had kicked in, someone had pressed play on the button marked TIME, *Do not pass GO, do not collect two bits*, and I had spent way too many years snuggled in the tattered nest with these other bewitching fowl and not honing my survival skills.

Someone had shaken the snow globe. This is not where I got off the bus at all. When did it slip away from me? Was I not paying attention? How did I not feel the plate tectonics?

One day, I walk through the pounding circus of my city and it creepily dawns on me. I feel like the creature from long ago, the coelacanth swimming in the lagoon of spangly reef fish. How did it all become so puzzling? Where did my city and its dwellers go?

Some weeks later, I venture out again, and once more, the rug had been pulled out from under me, the room rearranged, and the understudies have all taken over. Who's been playing musical chairs in my absence?

It's not as if I can re-live that past even if it were to suddenly resurrect in a new body, or a different time, or another place. Nothing escapes the fusillade, does it? One day, as it always does, it happens. The center, already soft, shaky and chewy, just cannot hold any more poop.

One morning, I just could not put up with having one more crackhead camped out on the front stairs, swaying his head in the smoke-ring clouds billowing from his crack pipe which looks suspiciously like my truck's radio antenna, not another protracted spell of wheezing and coughing and hacking up sputum all over the take-out menus. One day I wake up and I realize I can no longer climb Meat Mountain at Hahn's Hibachi. I can make a valiant attempt but the best I can muster is Base Camp Five, the Kal-Bi Super Combo Special; which is neither Super nor Special since it only contains two animal species whereas "super" calls for a minimum of four, and "special" calls for six, at least.

Some weeks ago, someone defecated on the side of my apartment building, and then some animal pooped right squarely on top of the pile of shit. I'm guessing a cat, though a raccoon might also be possible. A squishy hazelnut brown patty on top of the choco-brown curled pile. At one time, I would have thought this was so damn cool; I would have taken Polaroids of it and showed everyone the sculptural effects, I would have postulated about the theories of abjection in art and culture. But now, I just want any one of my neighbors to wash that damn thing away before someone else poops on the existing totem. No one washed the poop away. And yes, the next day, there was another layer to the totem. And the day after, another.

Still, nothing familiar stirred in me. Not even a shitstack could prod a nostalgic ping out of me. I was gone.

I have less patience to suffer fools willingly anymore. This makes dating in the city a sheer challenge. Matters are not helped by my underdeveloped social skills and inept grooming sensibilities.

It's been years since I've mustered the balls or the heck to go out to the discotheque, and it's not even called that anymore. Not since dancing got so damn complicated and I inevitably end up looking like the lost *Solid Gold* dancer, the one who's escaped from the island where they've been banished. (It's an island like Dr. Moreau's and every *Solid Gold* dancer has a miniature version of his or herself who lives on a small column doing Debbie Allen-esque *Solid Gold* jazz dances to power ballads only they and their intended victims can hear in their heads.) I always feel disconcerted in bars. I never mastered the art of street cruising, or even the intricate techniques of flirtation in its minor and major scales and arpeggios. Being a soggy ball of crankiness and wearing my heart on my sleeve as if some emo bomb just exploded certainly does not help things. And in all honesty, in most of my waking life, I'm just crushed by a terrifying discomfort of being in my own skin whenever I am in public.

And then, there's *booty*. And then there is booty. When the time comes, and it will for everyone I'm certain, when you have to choose between sex and dignity, go with dignity. Unless, of course, – and here you get to fill in the blank with whatever you want.

I confess. I don't have sexual fantasies any more, not like I did when I was a pup. And such terribly elaborate and dirty ones they used to be, too. These days, I seem to have a lot of domestic fantasies. In 78 percent of those fantasies, the object of my affection is an ex-boyfriend. In almost all of those fantasies, he's wearing much better clothes than he does in real life. In one version of that daydream, we raise kids together; in one, we have a farm or a sprawling mansion; in another, we care for elderly parents; and in another, I die á la Ali McGraw in *Love Story* or Elsa the Lion in *Born Free*; and in yet another, we plan our big gay wedding. In one version of that wedding, I've concocted a snowstorm of gardenia petals inside the church as a surprise; in another, Tony Bennett sings at the reception. And in yet another, Shakira performs. She was so blond.

There used to be an old disco stomper, "So Many Men, So Little Time." Now, it's So Many Issues, So Little Time. I used to make fun of people with issues. Ha ha, I said. But now, I have them, I have issues. I have whole subscriptions. And I have arthritis. I have a pile of bills to pay, obligations to fulfill. I have a liver that is slowly turning to mush. I have my weaknesses whose hungers must be fed. I have all this chaos in my veins. I have half a tank of gas but I'm sure it's enough to get me to where I want to go.

At the end of Edith Wharton's *The House of Mirth*, the heroine who has lost all hope of knowing herself, of finding love or even settling, crumples onto the floor and wails, "I've tried so hard, but life is difficult, and I am a very useless person."

I am a useless person and I am content to lay in bed with the cat watching nine continuous hours of the Food Network or the *Top Chef* marathon on Bravo. And I'd say things to her like "Omigawd, Decat, did you see that? They've just marinated the sesame seeds and stuffed them into the asparagus, which they've lightly blanched and seasoned with the oils from crushed lemongrass and infused with just a tiny drop of mirin; then they've stuffed all that into a snapper which has been rubbed with handfuls of minced Korean ginger root and drizzled ever so lightly with light soy sauce and just three drops of that 75-year-old balsamic; then all of that is stuffed into a game hen whose cavity has been brushed with truffle oil and powdered liberally with Ras el Hanout, and then the whole thing is wrapped with slices of pancetta and its all going to salt-bake in a big hole in the backyard filled with red hot Bolivian lava rocks and salt from the Caspian Sea. Oh no! They're going to sous-vide the whole thing in someone's bathroom sink apparently, what a twist! Isn't that clever?"

Then I'd grab the cat's head and make her nod as if she was saying, "Yes! Yes! That is ingenious, I wouldn't have thought of doing that to snapper because I don't have opposable thumbs, can I have my Science Diet Lo-Cal kibble now?"

My dear mom has a plan for me. It worked for my brother and so she thinks it might just work for me. Go With God! is the plan. On the eve of his wedding, my brother told me that Mom was always tormented by the idea that he might marry a bimbo. She decided to fast and pray for a week in supplication so that God would find a good wife for him.

I was the best man at my brother's wedding, I love my sister-in-law, I simply adore my little nieces to whom I am the wacky uncle who buys them amazing books and scads of completely impractical but absolutely fabulous presents.

I love my mom, she is so beyond PFLAG already. She's going to fast and pray to God, that's with a capital G, the Big Man as seen in the pages of the Holy Bible, Jehovah, Yahweh — the same God that Baptist conventioneers pray to in order to save the known Earth from wooly shit-stabbing perverts — and she's going to beseech Him to find me a partner. "I truly believe that God has a good man in store for you," she tells me. "And you know what would be nice?" she says, "It'd be so much better if you fasted and prayed at the same time with me!" Okay, that I can surely do.

Five days later, Mom calls and asks how my fasting and praying is going; she has been steadfast in her faith. At that moment when she called, I was sitting with a box of Popeye's Fried Chicken in my lap, watching Mixed Martial Arts on cable.

I like fried chicken because it is chicken, and it is fried.

Chapter 15, verse 34 of *The Gospel According to St. Mark* tells us that "at the ninth hour, Jesus cried with a loud voice, saying, 'Eloi Eloi, lama sabachtani?' which is interpreted, 'My God, my God, why hast thou forsaken me?'"

Life is difficult, and I am a useless, useless person. Look to the language, I've been told. But we all have the same language, used in the same epoch; we all have the same raw ingredients. Except some folks will make a lovely marinated smoked herring, to be served with a marsala custard on homemade pancakes. Some will make a good, filling unpretentious ham and cheese sandwich. And there are those content with an oily but tasty take-away with dubious nutritional value. And then there's McDonald's. This is why I hate cooking shows on television and why I love movies where the Amish fall in love; which is all neither here nor there, but I already told you I was useless.

I am checked into a room in the tower of Babel. It is a tall building with many rooms. I wander through hallways and corridors rushed with the colors and soundtrack to this life. Somewhere at this time, somewhere in the world, someone is falling in love to Sam Cooke crooning *That's Heaven To Me*, and here, in this one room, I will find my love. Here in this room, there is nothing that cannot be named, and nothing that needs to be. He speaks to me in barbed wire and I reply in gasoline. He kisses me fire-ragged and I smooch back lava-perfect. We crucify, we resurrect, we beloved, we end, we begin. We know. We tender. We open wide enough for birds to fly through and nest wherever they should desire. And in this one room, I know what it is to be happy.

I've been told that there is a Japanese word for something that is made more beautiful by its use. I know there is a French word for the trail a scent leaves in its wake. There is a Dayak word that could mean either nausea or affection, all depending on the context, tone, circumstance, and the relation between the speaker and the subject. That's the sort of guy I want to be when I'm tormented by love and its bafflements. But I don't even have the proper words to describe what I want to be, how pathetic is that? Love, that cocksucker. Oh, if only there was truth in naming.

I used to want a daddy. Now, I want a daddy to mother me.

I still sleep on one side of the bed. I still love the way guys smell. I still harbor in my heart something that resembles hope but is not it. And I still want to see the ending that has yet to been written.

I still want to be king.

And in spite of it all, I still do love my life in all its queer permutations. Even on the days when I so desperately want to be saved, even in the moments when I so direly need to be tamed, even at my lowest crush, I still do honestly love my life. And saying that I love my life is not the same as saying that I expect any happiness from it.

Queen

The Cock of Last Resort. I am in an alleyway, a basement let-in, the leather blindfold firmly in place, gripping my eyes until I can feel the moist condensation of sweat between the fragrant leather and my short-sighted eyes. The puffy eye pads press into my eyeballs so tightly that I see green and purple phosphenes as if I were on acid watching a Grateful Dead lightshow but there are no unwashed hippies here, no skanky flower-children that never grew up nor teenage converts to the nostalgia trip, just the sound of shoes and boots scuffling around me, flies unzipping, the smack of cocks in hand, the ale smell of crotches and unwashed pubes, the occasional grunt and cough, the sticky smack of semi-dried lubricated cocks against flesh. *The Cock of No Contest.* There are those who will grab your head and there are those who will grab your ears like a teapot short and stout. There are those who will hold your shoulders and those who will try to reach down and pinch your nipples. There are those who you will feel nothing but their cocks in you as they are busy pinching their own nipples as hard as they can. Then there are those who have absolutely no idea what to do with their hands. *The Cock of Dreams.* Cocks fill my mouth, caress my tongue, poke blindly at my lips, slap against my cheeks, one by one they drip their load into my face, in my hair, dribbling down my chin, down my throat, on my lips, on my tongue, and I take it in like so many deep breaths, the last gasp of a drowning dog. The very first time I had a cock in my mouth, I gagged so hard, I vomited so much I scared myself. The man fled the toilet stall. At that moment I decided that I will never gag again, no matter how large or mean or deep the next cock got. I practiced with fat marker-pens, broom handles, shampoo bottles, beer bottles, carrots, cucumbers. I practiced on the dog to make sure that I could tolerate even the most disgusting cock. I practiced hard and, like musicians training for the symphony, I got to Carnegie Hall. *The Cock of Wine & Roses*. Once I was falling so fast that I woke up in a pool of piss. Once I was falling and when I woke I was falling and when I got up, I was still falling. There is a guy that I meet with sometimes, our relationship is wholly undefined, he is not a hustler, at least not in my eyes, but someone I pay. Not necessarily with money. But that is a different story altogether. We agree on a number and it is his job to get me that number of loads. We use dice for this, sometimes one die, sometimes two. He blindfolds me and puts my wrists and ankles in shackles and ties me to the bed, he puts a gag in my mouth, he saves his load for the last one of the session. In the meantime, he gets on the phone and calls phone-sex lines and party-room conferences, he gets on the computer hook-up sites and invites anyone to come and feed me. He takes pictures of the men who come through to feed me. I know, I can hear the click and whirls of the Polaroid camera, I can see the flash through the edges of the blindfold. After the session, after he empties his cock into my mouth, he unshackles me and holds me while I cry like a whipped child. He whispers into my ear, describing the men who I have eaten from. He never shows me the pictures though, in my imagination, I like to think that he masturbates to them in private, maybe he sells them to other people, saying, "Look, here's a picture of a pig, a real pig, (oink! oink!) do what you want to do to him, here's his address." *The Cock of Understanding.* When did you learn how to suck cock? The artist Louis Nevelson was once asked how she created her art, and she replied in her croaky Bette Davis voice, *Honey, how do you eat a peach?* Sucking cock is nothing like eating peaches. It is nothing like sucking even as the prominent verb/continuous tense of its namesake suggest. Suck: To draw into the mouth by inhaling; to draw from in this manner; to draw in by or as if by suction; to suckle. In my youth, terrified by the crudeness and suggestiveness of language, we called it "eating ice cream." But it is nothing like eating ice cream at all. It is nothing like breathing, it is nothing like art. It is its own act, its own tense, transitive verb, noun, dangling pronoun. Oh, how it dangles. It is its own universe, not made of atoms but of stories, so many stories you wish you were deaf. *The Cock of Love.* Once, I considered pulling all my teeth out. I had met a man who promised me nothing but load after load of jism from his beautiful cock and I had partaken of it enough to believe him, it was his suggestion. The gum job, the selling point men who have gotten so decrepit that that's the best they can offer on phone-sex lines, sight unseen, all that's known is a mouth, void of teeth, just a fleshy wet slobber to face-fuck. I chickened out at the last minute. Or maybe I was never going to do it anyway. More likely, I couldn't make the sacrifice of having a wound in my face, unable to suck cock for weeks while it healed. "Sucking cock has nothing to do with monogamy," I recall being told and I got on my knees in the backroom of another bar and I never ever saw that man again. It is no loss. Not yet. *The Cock of First Offense.* There are two kinds of hell. One is an icy world where sinners are lodged in a lake of ice, their heads two-thirds popped out of the glassy sheet, mouths trapped beneath the frozen solidity, the air dry as meat lockers. In the other, the more common version, hell is the fire and brimstone land that children are told they will be sent to if they misbehave, don't obey, or tell family secrets. Here, demons rip out the glutton's bowels and drape their intestines on pine trees that are on fire. Liars are fed hot coals. Idolaters have their eyes poked out with blunt pencils. Those who love gossip have their eardrums perforated with biting insects. We're told it is the hottest place that anyone will ever experience. The hell you want to go to, though, is that place somewhere between the two hells. Here, there is no sand, as all the sand has melted into glass. But unlike the fiery hell where sand melted into glass remains in liquid puddles collected on the floor like clogged storm drains in the Mission, rank and foul-smelling, floating with the flotsam of discarded memories, the melted sand in this place turns into a sparkling expanse of glass that you may walk on. It is like walking on an eternal sheet of shattered windscreens, cracked, shattered as an exquisite spider web but still holding to each chip, smooth as the underbelly of lizards, the size of the desert. The fierce light from the Fiery Hell and the coldest intense light from the Ice Hell light this place and the waves of light sneak through the cracks in the glass and make it radiate into a quintillion spray of light. It is a hell worth going to. *The Cock of Heaven & Earth.* Someone's beeper goes off, someone is chatting to another in the background, someone is preparing for another shot, someone pops open a canned drink, someone can't get hard, someone has the cold flaccidity of a tweaker, someone I recognize, someone has brought a friend, someone is being reacquainted, someone has a new piercing, someone has a fever, someone has strange bumps on his cockhead, someone is severely deformed. This is democracy in action. I take it all. I accept it all. I accept them all. Like a mother of a nation, I hold them all dear to me. Here on my knees, in this alley, this basement let-in with this blindfold in place, here at the wee hours of a new dawn, week after week, month into years, I am queen, and I will rule here forever and ever. Watch my coronation, watch me ascend the throne.

Bolster

Things That Convey Hope, or The Possibility of
Happiness Forthcoming

The morning after; One more spin, once more around, one more;
"Don't you pay them no mind"; The brief window the newly in-love
find where they are shown who they should be; Proceeding with
the day even while knowing that the other will cancel or simply
not show, which does happen, and does not; The director asking,
"How many props are necessary to pull off sorrow?"; Google-ing
'insomnia' in the middle of the night; From which altitude one
looks like a weed in a field of weeds, an ineloquent dot asleep
in a dream; The passage of time, the passing of life, the days, the
countless hours and minutes and seconds, the sweep of the clock's
second hand; The glass half empty or half full in the dishwasher.

* * *

Are we made of stories or are we made of facts?

And which builds better? The stories of evidence and archive, or the ones built from each living and dying cell of your body?

The story of a life is constructed together in relationships. The people close to us — family, friends, lovers, colleagues, enemies even — become the mirrors and journals in which we recall and inscribe our history, they are the instruments that help us know ourselves and remember ourselves; and we do the same for them.

But stories wear out, erode. You leave them behind — in an old apartment, under the sink, in the back of a cab squashed between the seat cushions. Or the story loses its legs, its lungs; the meaning holding it aloft wavers, flinches too much, gets outdated. Over time, you become someone else. The story suffers from too much light, too much darkness, from the constant poking and peeling, over familiarity.

And what is left but all those dark eyes staring back at us. Look at the pictures, look in the archives, look in the footnotes, look at the souvenirs. Look in the mirror, in all the reflective surfaces.

* * *

THINGS ONE MIGHT TAKE TO BE A SIGN OF GREAT MEANING & SIGNIFICANCE BUT ARE REALLY UNREMARKABLE & INCONSEQUENTIAL

Double rainbows; Two-headed calves; Feral parrots rousting in the palm trees at first light; Butterflies at night; A long shriveled plant coming back to life; Seeing the number 11 or 1's and zeros in various permutations; Finding pennies on the street or in cracked spaces; Dreams where avifauna speak to you; Dreams of financial riches; All nightmares induced by eating Mission burritos before bedtime; Roadkill.

* * *

What happens after "Goodnight"? What happens after the bedtime story?

We imagined apocalypse because it was easier than the complicated futures that lay ahead. A future fraught with baffling new technologies, impenetrable financial power structures, ever shifting alliances and collapsing social systems, perplexingly malevolent microorganisms, and a language devolving and impotent. Death was more imagineable than the person that all the decisions and burdens of adulthood and survival would make of us. Charging bullishly into life with all barrels loaded without the fear of consequences was an act of desperation, though at the time some might have mistaken it for fearlessness, youthful prerogative, or selfish immaturity. It was a declaration that there were more terrible things than death; there were desires so urgent — for anesthesia, distraction, the dark brooding forces of need, the quelling of survivor's guilt; there were corrections so grave to undertake — the defying of fate's gauntlet, the dissent against conformity and apathy, the mutiny against the downward spiral of despair and our inherited pessimism.

Gambling, drug taking and love were our rituals of hope.

But all hope suffers from its own insufficiency.
Failure was our tutor and guide, was what we mostly learnt from.

* * *

You spend your life as an activist, an artist, a diva, or a slut, and then you're the box of your coffin, the box of your columbarium, the box of ashes, the box of papers and artifacts sitting on a shelf.

And you think about all the boxes you've tried to write and live yourself out of, and all the boxes other people have tried – successfully or un – to herd you into, and the boxes that you willingly climbed into, all the boxes you've struggled against, or made cozy with.

Funny isn't it, how everyone believes themselves to be "out of the box" thinkers? You don't ever hear anyone declaring, *I think inside the box.* Maybe in-the-box types aren't given to making declarations about themselves; they would have to think outside the box to do that.

Then there is the other box, the more prurient one: the ones you really wanted to get into, and your own which you'll gladly fold the flaps out open for whomever.

Does all living lead into a box of some sort? Is it futile to think that one is ever free of the box? Hey, so… why is the mime trapped in a box? No, seriously, this is not a set-up for a punchline. Why is the mime trapped in a box? Of all the standard mime tricks, this one stands apart.

The wall is understandable, we fall walls everyday of our lives. People pull on rope all the time, they climb ladders, they lean against things, they lift stuff, they eat sloppily. All these are common everyday acts, rooted in their normalcy, you may find yourself doing any one of these things. You may even find yourself struggling against the wind with your umbrella on some stormy day. But how often does one find oneself stuck in a box?

And it's a box. It's not all that sturdy. Even if you're stuck in a high-class box, it's still cardboard. But even if it were wooden, if you push against it, brace and bare against the sides, it'll come apart. If you're trapped in a cardboard box and are too weak and puny to push your way out, just take a piss and it'll sag and come apart.

* * *

Things That Sound Delightfully Obscene but Aren't At All

Tittle, Umlaut, Glottal, Cockmaster, Titchy, Sloppy, Lorem Ipsum.

* * *

Things That Sound Delightfully Obscene but Aren't Even When They Are

Jarns, Nittles, Quimps, Grawlix.

* * *

There is a kind of euphoria in grief, a degree of madness, unspoken and unacknowledged, an undercurrent that fueled the survivors.

This was a time when we still grieved in our own rooms, real or imagined, shared or squatted. We valued and stubbornly held on to the dignity we could feel slipping away. This was a time when we still had our private lives. When being a shameless whore or hussy was an action deliberately taken. It was beautiful work and the quality of the shamelessness, the effrontery of the brazenness, was all the more richer and dazzling for the effort put behind it.

None of that national mourning, that showy community grieving that we find so commonplace these days. None of those garish roadside shrines, each one competing with the next for more stuffed animals, more plastic flowers, more ink-jet printed photos, or in a brilliant trumping move, stuffed animals and plastic flowers together encased in a balloon held aloft by a plastic rod.

Real Simple magazine would recommend Ash (home-ground, of course) and Sackcloth (easily home-rendered as well.) It's all you need.

Many years ago, a neighbor back home had died and the wake was held in the house's living room. Every day for a week, in the evening, a small silver van would pull up and a group of black clad women would get out of the van and proceed into the house. And then it began. The loudest, wailing-est, most screeching and terrifying screams and sobbing and crying ever heard. Professional mourners. Every day from 6 p.m. to 7 p.m., except for Friday and Saturday which was from 1 p.m. to 2 p.m. Sunday was a day off, of course. And at 7 p.m. or 2 p.m. on the dot, the bawling stopped as instantly as it started, as if someone had pressed the STOP button on the stereo, as if there was a conductor leading an orchestra to its final coda. Then the ladies would file out, clutching onto their handkerchiefs or tissues in one hand, with a can of soda or Orange Crush in the other, and pile into the van and off they went to the next gig.

That is how it should be done. That is the job I would most like to have.

* * *

AIDS Drugs That Sound Like Hipster Baby Names

Isentress; Sustiva; Truvada; Kaletra; Prezista; Reyataz; Selzentry; Lexiva; Ziagen; Zerit; Entriva.

"Don't mind her, Kaletra is very mature for her age, aren't you sweetie?"

"Isentress and Prezista have been raving non-stop about theatre camp..."

"QiGong classes have really helped Lexiva and Ziagen to balance out their ADHD."

* * *

The thing about activism is that so very often one ends up advocating on behalf of people who one just doesn't quite care for. People who grate upon your very being. Perhaps they'll mock your dedication, your hard selfless work; perhaps they'll live their lives that will set the movement back tens of years, people who simply just aren't helping. These people's lives would be greatly enhanced and enriched by your sweat and stress and commitment to social justice even as they support causes and positions abhorrent to you.

Yes, yes, no man is island; yeah, yeah, butterfly flapping wings; uhhuh uhhuh, greater humanity, greater good…

At some point, you will realize that you are not one of your heroes. You are something else altogether and you have to take that into consideration.

* * *

We were past the awful crushing '80s, death and day-glo, the dead were leveling off in the city and soon there would even be a week followed by more weeks where there was not one obituary in the fag-rags, which was some kind of minor miracle it seemed. The awful toxic medications had been reformulated to resemble something that could even pass for compassion. A stride had been struck, a pace brokered. Those with the wherewithal had managed to deftly work the red tape of SSI and disability and an assortment of city and state benefits into a nice trust fund from Uncle Sam. Not quite the level of the Rockefellers or the Hiltons, but enough to live their quirky, queer lives that everyone seemed to have hobbled together from thrift store bargains, temp jobs, and all the moxie of the beautifully worthless, the diseased nothings.

Soon, the pile of pills we had in hand would become a different pile of pills. This time, with the power to drag that unswerving line of light into a prism to refract into a thousand pieces and points, except it wasn't a prism glass but some old piece of glass, perhaps a chipped piece of windscreen, or a broken award trophy, found by the road.

Little did we know but we each were the guinea pigs of the other. Our benevolent inquisitors, clipboards in hand, starched concern botoxed in their faces, recorded and collated and compiled, how much, how long, how wrong, when then, what happened, what failed irrevocably, what next.

The prospects weren't quite that gleaming and sunshiny, though it was soon to be, but we couldn't have known that just yet. Nor could we fathom how astonishing it would be. We lived in the eternal present. We had to think like heroes, superheroes even, in order to be mere decent human beings.

We could not know if there was something better over the hill or not, but that didn't matter because we had our friends and lovers marshaled. And we had something that resembled hope and could very well have been it, albeit tattered and gimpy and effete.

* * *

40 NAMES

Are they online usernames from M4M4Sex – or – actual Chinese restaurants from the southern and midwestern United States?

1. TastyTop
2. Hungry1
3. BigWong
4. Chopstix
5. BlueDragon

6. JoyLuck
7. YellowRiver
8. Chinamax
9. ChinaBear
10. ChinaMaster
11. Nuthuggers
12. HotWings
13. GreenBamboo
14. HoHo
15. RiceBowl
16. Chinex
17. Eggroll
18. PanDa
19. Wok&Chops
20. Noodling
21. RiceLovers
22. Dumpling
23. Flaming
24. Fuffut
25. RiceFarm
26. YumMy8
27. JockMeat
28. LickMy7
29. GoldenCocks
30. MushuU
31. Prime8
32. Irishwasabi
33. shakeit
34. TopMission
35. Xlgmeat
36. APlusTop

* * *

Things I Didn't Know I Loved

Silence, Solitude, Uncomplicatedness, The Desert (as much as the sea), Mornings (as much as nights), Winter storms, Home.

* * *

I used to live in the apartment beneath Junior Miss Speedfreak Northwest 1987. It's such a trite cliché that it embarrasses me somewhat to even mention it, but it seemed as though she had not stopped vacuuming for four days — the whirr of some household appliance bumping into furniture and walls was a constant. And when she wasn't vacuuming, she would be washing the pavement with the Wondermop™ that she obviously bought from an early morning infomercial, a product I too on certain aimless occasions had desired to possess. Some early mornings, I would peel back my curtains and she would be smoking in front of the apartment building with her mop, her oily acne-spotted cheeks shining in the last glows of the streetlamp's halogen dying flare. You almost expect to see the lit tip of that cigarette inch into her oil-trap face and ignite into a pyre. She was harmless enough, and we all left her to her vices, ignoring her endless stream of boyfriends who visited at all hours of the night while she vacuumed. At least our sidewalk was spotless. Even in the fall, not one dried leaf was to be found on our block of sidewalk, it was as if the path was Scotchgarded. Then, one day, she stopped vacuuming and stopped mopping, the whirr wound down its humming decibels, her boyfriends stopped coming around, and eventually, when no one was looking, and no one was ever looking despite her persistent paranoid insistence that everyone was, she moved away. No one saw any moving trucks or her lugging any boxes out of the building. She just disappeared. The landlord showed up to inspect the place and found it bare, picked clean almost; he was expecting it to be trashed. And after a few hours, the pavements grew dusty and stained again. Someone said that maybe she got clean, tripped on her hideous oversized bell-bottoms and face-planted straight down that flight of twelve steps. I miss having a clean pavement, however unnatural it looked.

I once witnessed a Buddhist wake — or was it Taoist? I'm never quite sure — where the mourners, paid and real, stayed up all night playing cards, eating and drinking and gambling and keeping watch over the casket. The wake spilled out of the house and into the driveway, crept out of the garage and onto the sidewalk and street, all lit by the harshest fluorescent lights and perfumed with unflinching incense and cigarette smoke. The assorted family members, mourners, and funeral workers gathered at the tables laid out for the funeral dinner and gambled all night. I longed to sneak into the wake but I didn't need to. It was open to anyone, just as long as there was no disrespecting the deceased or the mourning family. I ended up in a gorgeous marathon mah-jong session, lost $217 when day finally broke, and as one shift of weary gambling mourners filed away to finally go to sleep, content with their duty to the deceased, and another shift arrived to take their place, I was left with the most beautiful ache in my gums and jaw from my sleep deprivation and all the second-hand smoke.

Stay awake, by sheer will. Stay awake.

I am awake. Sleep creeps on me like some snaking demon vine. I go out walking way past midnight. What I like about the city is that it is grid out, main drag crisscrossing main drag. But between these there are smaller, narrow side streets that break away from the rush of the drag, capillaries that break away from the main choke and rush, forging a different life at its own speed, but still remembering to keep pace with its source. Walking in the early hours of morning is a sleepless pleasure. The streets are quiet, there are few vehicles. The street people and the homeless have bedded down for the night. Neighborhoods in the day and the rambling night pegged as dangerous and grimy are now deserted and as safe as your grandmother's driveway. This world is quiet, but people are always there. Midnight tweakers and bar dregs, people who have normal middle-class and working-class lives are folks crawling in the gutters of need. Kids, teenage fixers. The working classes who need to open shop, to start machines, to prepare for the day, the ones who work in time zones hours ahead, the shift-changers, the over-timers.

The things you see, the music you hear. The sensation of the material world as it grazes against your skin. Everything is intensified, as if you were jellyfishing through a dream-like ocean world, a psychedelic sea ruddered by nothing but your spiny body. Everything is haloed, every color saturated, every dimension and ratio intensified. The sounds, so white noise, are retuned on an expanding 32-note scale. Voices Stradavarius on angelic overtones as if you were walking through a version of heaven of your own and best creation and orchestration.

Stay awake. I want to stay awake.

My early dawn strolls down side streets became my grammar, my secret blood. And I know what I was seeing, what I had seen, all that I knew. In my mind, I saw myself become a pulsating figure, glowing like the day of rapture. The street was where I was found, was my love, was a corridor of endless doors, and the surface of the tarmac gleamed as if paved with Parisian cobblestones, and I was my own angel, my swan, as beautiful as any dark sweetness.

Stay awake. The flicker in any given ordinary life lures. No matter what or where the flickering points to, where it emanates from, it's all triggered against such the beautiful naptime. Stay awake. My thoughts were never clearer, I never knew as many things as I did in those days of nights. I knew blood.

I am awake, the last day of my future, the first day of my past. I am awake and I've been awake. I am wide open and I don't believe I shall ever close or fold ever again.

* * *

Things I Know I Appreciate

Two-ply toilet paper; Stoicism; The nature of cats; Good food in good company; Good books; Common sense; The subtleties and contradictions, the ridiculousness and ironies, the surprises and perfections that lay like bear traps in any life; Time of my own; A finely aged and hard-earned cynicism, one that hasn't yet turned bitter or festered into meanness; Kindness (of strangers and not strangers).

* * *

Side Effects

Headache, nausea, vomiting, diarrhea, stomach pain, muscle pain, fatigue, insomnia, blood in urine, dark urine, pale stools, chest pains, dizziness, fever, chills, sore throat, increased urination or thirst, irregular heartbeat, numbness, tingling, trouble breathing, unusual bruising or bleeding, swelling of the mouth and lips, hives or rashes, skin blisters, weight loss, kidney problems, seizures, depression, suicidal ideation, fainting, excessive hunger, pancreatitis, jaundice, extreme anemia, hepatitis, male infertility, drug-induced Lupus, severe anorexia, renal papillary necrosis, vertigo, tinnitus, psychosis, phototoxicity, vaginal discharge or irritation, hallucinations, death.

* * *

He said:

Can you imagine if they found a cure? Can you imagine that? What would happen? For one, this whole freaking city would fall apart. Do you know how many people would be out of a job? How many non-profits and their directors and staffs would be dumpster-diving for their dinners? With medical practice insurance the way it is, and with lawsuits the way they are, would your physician ever admit to having made a mistake, even one that was unintended?

If they need your diseased body to maintain their livelihood, to justify their salaries, to fuel their grant applications, can you trust that they'll tell you the truth?

* * *

He said:

I think this is a matter of moral statement than a public health one. Or even a rational one. (picks up the pamphlet and reads) *The risk for STDs is directly related to the number of sex partners you have: The more sex partners, the greater the risk of contracting it. Having more sex with fewer partners reduces your risk of getting STDs.* Let's look at it this way: If I have sex with 200 men, absolutely dirty sex with 200 men, each of whom do not have syphilis, would the risk still be greater than if I had sex with just one guy who has syphilis?

She said:

Sir, you're being difficult. Now tell me the names of those 200 men.

* * *

I'm a great believer of lying in one's journal. It's the one place where you can lie with impunity. If you suspect anyone is going to read your journals, you should lie even more spectacularly. Just make sure it's plausible. I'm not a journal type of guy. I have notebooks, I take notes, even though the half-life of my handwriting is about 14 hours. But as far as a journal diary where daily or every few days I'd record what happened to me, and my feelings and thoughts about it, that's not for me. Don't have the discipline, don't have the bother, don't got the don't got. Reading someone else's journal is an odd enterprise. Even if you have the person's permission or, say, the person is dead and his journals are in a box somewhere and you are given access to it.

The immediate sense right off the bat is that you shouldn't, that you're somehow betraying a trust, invading a private boundary. That sense is quickly and easily chucked to the side by your salacious curiosity. Oh, what morbid and titillating secrets will you find? What ghoulish confessions will be revealed? The answer to that, almost always, is none. Nada. Not a damn thing.

It's go to work, come home, what I had for lunch, for dinner, what I need to do for work, for home, for self-improvement. Maybe Mom and Dad are visiting, I go on vacation and this is what I saw and Wow! Look at what I saw. I spy cute guy who doesn't know I'm alive. Someone asks me out on date, I go. Didn't work out. I ask someone out on date, Yay! He says yes! All atwitter date night. Didn't work out. I love my pets. I like my friends. This is my reaction to what is happening politically in my time, it's middle of the road, bootstraps and acculturation. If partnered, this is what my husband did, this is what pissed me off, this is what I did, this is our argument, these are our apologies and making up, and then the motherfucker did this again, argue argue, make up make up, I love him so much, go on vacation together, come home and break up. I miss him, I hate him, I love him but not in love with him, and these are the lessons I have learned.

And then there'll be all the entries where therapy sessions are recounted. Holy fuck, how much therapy can one person go through? My therapist said this. I am trying my therapist's suggestions. Putting into practice what I learned in therapy. I have therapy tomorrow, in two days, in two hours. My therapist said this. My therapist said that.

If, after the 8ᵗʰ journal, you're still whining about the same crap, you're either doing it wrong or you're a hopeless little turd. Or your therapist is.

The one who is having sexual relations with his therapist is unlikely to journal about it, because his therapist has likely convinced him not to, hence disposing of evidence, and also because he's too fucked up and too busy fucking up his life to take time out to journal. The slut's not journaling either. He's busy slutting. He is collecting pubes from each of his tricks which he obsessively and lovingly places in old apothecary bottles and labels. It's a different kind of journaling.

I once knew someone who took snapshots of each of his tricks' assholes. He compiled these photos in dozens of photo albums, the kinds with the puffy, hard cardboard, fake leather covers. This was before digital cameras, and he shot these with a regular 35mm camera, which meant that these rolls of film had to go somewhere to be developed. In this digital age, anytime you go online, on any hookup site, sometimes not even, you're simply confronted by greasy butthole shots, whether you want to look or not, even if you avert your eyes, they are there, waiting to slap you in the face like a clammy washcloth. So it's no small wonder that this man possibly had the largest collection of pre-digital greasy butthole shots in the world. Flipping through those albums, and when the pages were opened out end to end I remember thinking first that it looked not unlike the bed of coral reefs. Some pages later, it began to look like some meaty new wave paint chip sample, a color wheel of browns, pale orange earthtones, and mauve that you wouldn't want on any wall. This man that I knew also happened to die very suddenly of a heart attack. And it was left to his college-aged twin sons from an earlier, straighter life to come and clean out his downtown apartment. I'm sure there's a story in there somewhere, I just don't want to look.

Of the personal diary, poet Adam Zagajewski writes that they are often "uncommonly irritating — as it should be" with its "extreme narcissism" and "ill humor," adding that the diary that "doesn't bother everyone is one that has clearly been falsified." In thumbing through modern day journals, one thing in common reveals itself: the last entry is simply an abrupt drop, a page of a day hanging in mid-air, like in cartoons when the ground has vanished under the character's feet. And the poor thing is standing there with a gorblock expression on his face before he plummets.

No one journals right up to the bitter end. I'm certain it's because by then the shit has certainly hit the fan and is pinwheel splattering the room. The run up to that is likely spent dealing with a whole hog of issues, medical or otherwise, and taking care of business, loose ends, all ends to the end.

Reading that last page, you sense that the person is still unaware of what's coming up ahead around the bend. And even if they know they're chronic, that last page still is unaware of the time line. The stopwatches ticking, the alarm clock with the snooze button pried off.

* * *

The new meds gave a new lease on life to many who had decidedly checked out or were prepared to. Going into overtime, the next round, the sequel. Would we be so gauche as to call it 'sudden death'?

* * *

This one was about to sit for his real estate license. This one would do something at Franklin Templeton. This one and this one only wanted nothing more than academia, to be absorbed into the post-graduate miasma. This one returned to the Midwest never to be heard from again. This one got married and had four kids and a life down low. These ones moved to the suburbs for their techie jobs and turned to fungus. This one turned to fungus right where he was. This one moved to New York and made it big. This one moved to Los Angeles and gave up. This one got all corporate. This one jumped off the Golden Gate Bridge. This one hung himself. This one got sober, then not, then again. This one moved back home to take care of his mom. This one became a born-again Mormon. This one became a porn star, which is to say he acted in some porn movies. This one got 10 to 15 years in San Quentin. This one always had his eye on higher political office and his plan was right on track. This one sought a higher spiritual existence. This one drank the Kool-Aid, and this one sold the farm twice over. This one everyone wished well, said with an eye-roll or two.

And then there was the one who told everyone that he was the Crown Prince of the Sultanate of Johore in Malaysia. The one who said he was the grandson of Akio Morita. The one who said his family owned Catalina Island. The one who said he was head of security detail for George Michael. The one who sold his story to the *National Enquirer*. The one who waited for his lawsuit to pay off, and waited. The one who married up and across and diagonally. The one who achieved some measure of fame from starring third fiddle in a successful network TV series, though few believed him even as the series ran for twelve seasons. The one who was a cop, a paramedic, a surgeon, an oncologist, a pediatrician, a pharmacist, a guru, a lobbyist, a firefighter, an award-winning chef, a professional lesbian. The one whose family connections were a source of great bragging and embarrassment. The one who lied so beautifully you would watch in awe with the fire extinguisher in hand ready to douse his flaming pants.

* * *

Disturbing & Unsettling Snatches of Conversation Overheard at a Sex Party

"I don't want to go home to your toys..."; "...mostly single..."; "... fuck my angry he-cunt..."; "...what should we do with the body?..."; "...start wiping off fingerprints..."; "...accidentally shit myself behind the..."; "...my therapist says it's okay..."; "...stop touching me..."; "...oh, I'm still in high school...".

* * *

To exist in a time that is not the tragic heroic AIDS '80s, where the density of your grief and sorrow can wipe your slate clean, that what you experienced, what you saw, lived through — no matter how many degrees separated, no one will ever question you now — was enough to give you a free pass, a laminated card marked Redemption.

This was not the future yet fully emerging either, the new golden rainbow era of rights, relationships, optional closets, of acceptance, apathy, and a six-lane mainstream highway, all built on a history and struggle fast receding in the back distance. The rallying howls, the rebel yells, the wailing keen of the fallen all caught is a decrescendo. Don't look back or you'll turn salty.

This was neither nor the distance between them, but an exhausted netherland where no one quite knew whether to go forward or backward or to stay put, to lay down and die or to lay down a stake, to remember or forget, to recreate awash in nostalgia or to create anew, the past packaged in matching luggage sets and stashed in storage, to create anew without the annoying tentacles of the past, as if that were ever possible.

* * *

"First, no, I did not get laid. Yes, I got too high and no, I did not have a pleasant evening. I went to check out the guy I was telling you about. Well, Mr. Italy came to me in a cab and wanted to go to another guy's home in the Outer Mission. We get there and that guy does not answer the door, so then Mr. Italy takes me back to the Westin Hotel where he decides that he does not want sex. So I traveled with this fool all over town and we get high and then he asks me to leave. I get home to find both Bobby and Ricky are gone and it makes me a nervous wreck because they have been up for days and Ricky already freaked out twice this morning about his illegal substance bag being hidden or taken by his other boyfriend, Lyle, or their roommate. I hate to say this, and I realize that it's probably drug-induced paranoia but these people have been too good to me to not have an ulterior motive. Drug dealing whores do not just adopt a homeless person, feed him, and support his habit for no reason, do they? Well, I am kinda hot though, so maybe... But really, this all is now a life I want no part of. I really can't understand how I became a puppet in this amateur drama production.

I am back in the big city. If you receive this on Friday morning before you leave for work, would you please text or call me as I would like to stop by for just a few seconds and drop off that one little package that I was short last time, and an extra one as well to say Thank You. I sincerely appreciate your coming to my assistance when I was so desperate. I am considerably better in my budget management skills and have a new job working for a private political consultant in Oakland. I started working today and am really enjoying it, although it was stressful and I did not exactly stay on top of things. I am just very grateful for having the opportunity to re-enter the workplace. Once again, thank you for assisting me and for being my friend at all times. I think you might be the longest lasting yet. Let me know when I might stop by.

I am doing very well. Thank you for your kind inquiry. I sincerely hope to be moving back to the South but the question is when. You see, over the past year I have lost my life savings, retirement, job, house, two pieces of rental property, and most importantly my family due to my many addictions. Now that I have a grip and have successfully completed eight months of harm management treatment, I feel certain it is only a mere matter of time before I get saturated with this chemical and give it up completely.

At seeing this consistency of improvement, I had a lengthy conversation with my best friend's partner. He has been dealing drugs in this city for 19 years but he is now too ill and is having to give up his business. And in 19 years, not one arrest! He has suggested that I take over his clients for as many months as necessary to recover my losses. (He projects 18 months.) By my calculations, he is clearing around $10,000 a week, tax-free, in cash and only has 10 to 15 major clients. It was amazing helping him count out $10,000 in $20 bills! Anyway, I would love to do this and in order to do so I am going to need a silent partner who backs 50 percent of the investment. Now, look, don't run off saying No right away! Here is the deal: I am going to sign a legal binding agreement between myself and this individual that reads as a signature loan guaranteeing the return of the investment in full as a minimum, and if the investment has not been repaid in three months' time, I am to begin paying back monthly installments of $300 until the loan is repaid in full. Furthermore, the investor will receive $3000 (retail) in product to hold as collateral. After the initial investment is paid in full, the investor will receive 30 percent of gross profits each week, which should average $3,000 a week, tax-free cash, for as long as I maintain the operation. I then have the option to sell the business at the 18-month mark and again at the 24-month mark with the first option going to the investor. This is an established business and has a good name among this crowd. I can't see anything going wrong and it is the only way to gain that kind of capital in that short a time. And to tell you the truth, I sort of like the risk!

I wanted to see if you would be interested in this opportunity. I would love to know that you, as well as I, are benefiting from this. To have an offer handed to me like this is unheard of! The investment is $5,000; so it would be an investment of $2,500 each. This is broken down to $1,500 for clients and $3,500 for inventory — which by the way is $10,000 in product. The silent partner's name, nor any portion of his or her identity, shall ever be revealed. Furthermore, the investor will not be responsible for any other duties other than light bookkeeping and will be allowed to purchase product at cost! Win-Win all around!

Please let me know what you think. I am so excited about the entire proposition. I also look forward to a time you and I can hook up again.

* * *

Places in Someone Else's Apartment One Ought not to Hide or Dispose of One's Used Syringes & Points

On top of the bathroom vanity; Between books on the bookshelf; Under the bed; In the cat litter box; In potted plants; In the drywall; Behind large heavy immovable furniture; In the cistern; Underneath the carpet in far corners of the room.

* * *

"We tell ourselves stories to live." So begins Joan Didion's brilliant essay, "The White Album." It's a line oft quoted by readers and writers and all manner of folk. Much less frequently quoted, however, are the final words of that essay, which read "...and writing has not helped me see it clearly."

But it did, of course.

We lie to ourselves and to others because lies make for some of the most entertaining and endearing and fantastic stories. The act is even built into the name of the enterprise: Fiction.

But as the writer says: I don't lie, I just stretch the truth.

We tell ourselves lies because we can. And because people believe us. A lie requires that belief, that paying trust. If someone knows you're lying, then it's a fail. It's then not so much a lie as it is a bland untruth, an inaccuracy, a downgrade.

See how this works in regular life: we are often told that smoking crystal meth turns the user into a "different person." Not quite as thrilling as *The Exorcist* unfortunately, not quite at all. It merely turns the user into someone he has long wanted to be, something he's thought about being and doing. But this way, with this rationale, an exit strategy is put into place, just in case.

Consider: in the long history of the drug, the "different person" that emerges is always either Criminal or Slut, or very often both. You'd think that for a drug that's been around for close to a century, that someone, just one person, might have turned into something interesting, like a world-class plate-spinning vaudeville act or a contortionist or the Vladimir Horowitz of the recorder or one of those clowns who does tricks with mathematics, or anything other than the criminal fuck-up who's about to steal your iPad after shagging you.

We tell ourselves lies because we are the only ones who can fool ourselves.

* * *

Things That Are Near, Yet Far

The end; The beginning; The reprieve.

* * *

Each week, we dutifully showed up and planted our scrawny butts in those pinching hard-backed folding chairs and plotted our bright and brilliant futures. Futures, most if not many, would not live to see. Our eyes watered and wavered away from the prize. If it was a stare-off, it wasn't much of one. It wasn't even a fierce glare. It was pinkeye, glaucoma, cataracts, retinitis, optical muscle fatigue, detached retinas, infected contacts, fungal growths, ever-growing blind spots, and eventually, blindness.

Everyone had a different stopwatch, each set to their own countdown. A whole room of ticking, seconds ticking away, ticking enough to be torture, enough to drive even the hardiest insane.

And then, time was up.

* * *

On *Project Runway* in the U.S., when dismissing a contestant, Heidi Klum says, "One moment you're in, the next you're out." (Which is much improved over the original: "One moment you're in, the next you're on a cattle train and off to the camps.")

On *Project Runway Canada*, when dismissing a contestant, Iman says, "You do not make the cut."

On *Project Catwalk*, when dismissing a contestant, Elizabeth Hurley first, then Kelly Osbourne says, "You do not measure up."

On *Project Runway Australia*, when dismissing a contestant, Kristy Hinze says, "Goodbye. And Good Luck."

From this, what can we deduce about the national character of these countries and cultures? Which then of these countries can we deduce to be the most civilized?

And why stop there, why not:

"Your hems are unraveling like your promise."
"Your A-line is D+."
"Your Sunday is longer than your Monday."
"Your dismal failures and lack of vision and creativity is the new black."

* * *

THINGS THAT ARE FAR, YET NEAR

The end; The beginning; The reprieve.

* * *

He said:

It's not difficult to see how we are where we are today. In the '90s, the influx of new HIV meds gave many folks a new door to open. Since one of the symptoms of this chronic illness is sheer fatigue, it's not surprising that some would resort to methamphetamines to get up and on with the day. Welcome to the world of suburban soccer moms and long haul truckers. Unfortunately, no one thought to mention that some protease inhibitors would up the level of methamphetamines introduced into one's bloodstream. See how this might spin awry? Actually, in Europe and Australia, this information was readily available, but here in the good ol' U. S. of A, not a peep. Still, the public health folks should get on their knees and thank the scourge of the meth epidemic for saving their bony butts. It was somewhere to pin the blame on other than their failed efforts. Everyone needs an evil all-powerful nemesis in order to maintain balance and most of all, appearances.

She said:

Oh fucking Christ! Are you all cracked out again?

* * *

Do you have any enemies? Are you anyone's enemy? What is your feeling on revenge? Given the opportunity without reprisals, would you? Is vengeance mine? or yours? What is your feeling about karma? Karma chameleon, you come and go? Eye for an eye? or Turn the other cheek? Cheek to cheek? or Tit for tat? Measure for measure? or Give an inch? Take the mile? or Stand your ground? Is forgiveness really divine? Can you forgive someone who doesn't believe he has wronged you? Can you forgive someone who hasn't asked for forgiveness? How many times can you apologize for the same wrongdoing? Divine retribution or Human payback? Forgive and forget? or Forget about it? Would you feel better if there were a punishment involved? Or would you just feel petty and spiteful? Hanging or Stoning? Caning or Beating? When is an apology not an apology? Is a reluctant apology or a mandated apology still good? Are you sure you're not just being overly sensitive? or petty? What can you not forgive? Is someone forgiving you now? Should you be forgiven? Are apologies ever enough? Look who's sorry now? Does sorry really seem to be the hardest word? What's your apology worth, really? Or your forgiveness, for that matter? Is the slate ever really wiped clean? Are you having an asthma attack?

* * *

No, IT IS NOT

Surreal; Kafkaesque; Epic; The least bit fair; The end of the world; What you need nor what you deserve; Untenable.

* * *

YES, IT IS MOST SURELY

Fucked up; A lovely day; A burden to bear, preferably in silence, definitely with dignity.

* * *

One day, you're walking home at the time when everybody else is going to work, your nether regions feeling all swampy and slightly sore. As you pass reflection after reflection of yourself on passing doors of buses, on storefront glass, on car windows, you realize that you're pushing fifty in a few years. And all the little piggies you're playing with are at least two decades younger than you are, and they have no idea how you are broken nor do you have any clue how they are broken. All you have in common is this cracked piggishness, that in and of itself is admittedly undeniably delicious, but borne from such different and divergent things.

And then you think that maybe you have the answers, some answers at least, some stab at answering what's going wrong, why it's all coming apart, all the what the hell's the matter questions. Not to say that your answers are in the ballpark of being correct, though they might be, but at the very least, they are plausible and they draw connecting lines where no one had thought to before, they suggest a possibility.

But by this time, no one is listening, no one is asking you anymore. No one sees you any more than a monster or a ghost, a lump in space and time, a problem, a workhorse, another one amongst the others.

* * *

I WOULD MOST CERTAINLY LIKE TO

Bend without fear of breaking, break without fear of judgment.

* * *

But I am a liar, a sinner, a barebacker, a drug user, a degenerate, a slut, a home wrecker, a bugger, a scoundrel, a hopeless delinquent, a sick fuck, a vile idiot, an abomination, a shit-eating punk, a psycho nutjob, a sociopath, a useless piece of trash, a bastard son-of-a-bitch good-for-nothing lowlife scumbag.

And you cannot, must not, believe anything — not a single word — that I say.

About the Author

Justin Chin was born in Malaysia, raised and educated in Singapore, shipped to the U.S. by way of Hawaii, and has resided in San Francisco for many years. He is the author of three books of poetry, all published by Manic D Press: *Bite Hard* (1997); *Harmless Medicine* (2001), a Bay Area Book Reviewers Association Awards finalist; and *Gutted* (2006), winner of the Publishing Triangle's Thom Gunn Award for Poetry. Squeezed in between these were two non-fictions: *Mongrel: Essays, Diatribes & Pranks* (St. Martins, 1999) and the ur-memoir, *Burden of Ashes* (Alyson, 2002).

In the '90s, Chin also led a double life as a performance artist: he created and presented seven full-length solo works around the U.S. He packed up those cookies in 2002 (with occasional relapses) and the documents, scripts, and what-heck from that period were published in *Attack of the Man-Eating Lotus Blossoms* (Suspect Thoughts, 2005).